THE REBEL'S MATE

THE BLUE SOLACE: BOOK SEVEN

C.W. GRAY

❀ Created with Vellum

SUGARWORM SYSTEM, ABOARD THE
BLUE ALBATROSS, EN ROUTE TO
PLANET RUEAL

*F*inn Sterling sat sideways in the captain's chair, legs hanging over one armrest. His pilot, Alluva, was the only crew member currently on the bridge.

"All I'm trying to say is this ship seriously kicks ass," Alluva said. The Siren's curled horns were bent over the controls as she worked through a simulation. "Our old one was nice and all, but this baby has three times the space. With our upgrades, she's a damn fine battlecruiser *and* transport."

Finn grinned. He liked the new ship too. After the last battle back home, Humans First's fleet was decimated. Finn and his personal crew had led an ambush to take control of HF's backup fleet, and Finn had gained a brand-new, sparkly ship.

"I wouldn't get too comfortable." Finn swung his feet. "We spend most of our time on the station, and the Blue Albatross will probably be repurposed when we get home."

Alluva sighed. "Ruin my fun why don't you?"

Finn snorted and his ears twitched. "Hey, I never get to sit in the captain's chair, so I'll miss it too."

"You only get the captain's chair when Captain Weber isn't here." Alluva's laugh was cut off by the vid-com signal. "Looks like we have a message coming in from Charybdis Station."

Finn quickly slid out of the chair and checked the time. "They're early. I'll take it in here instead of my office."

"Do I need to make myself scarce?" Alluva asked.

"No, just lock the bridge doors." Finn sat back down and did his best to look serious and official, his tail tucked around him.

The Lord Admiral's purple fuzzy face appeared on one screen while the Blue General and the newly appointed Vice Admiral appeared on other screens.

Lord Admiral Fasi Juren grinned at him. "You look good sitting in that seat, Finn."

Finn stroked the armrests. "I make anything look good."

"Don't get used to it." Blue General Hackett raised a brow. "You're my lieutenant, and I'm not letting you get away."

Finn rolled his eyes. "Yeah, yeah."

Vice Admiral Draif Ando hid a grin. "Anyway, we called early for a reason."

"What's happening?" Finn relaxed back in his seat and tucked a leg under him. "We reach Rueal tomorrow, and so far, my fleet hasn't had any problems along the way."

"That's good to hear." Fasi looked thoughtful. "While HF's fleet is destroyed and their leadership dead, there will be lower-level supporters out there. We don't expect any trouble from them, but they could be a hindrance."

Finn knew his grin looked a little feral since his sharp incisors bit into his lip. "They can try to stop me all they want."

Hack smirked. "That's my lieutenant. Give them hell."

Finn would love the chance. A few months ago, President Wineon, the former leader of Vextonar, sold over half of the population of her planet into slavery to help fund Humans First. By the time she was finished, the only people left on Vextonar had either been a slave or at least seventy-five percent human.

"How's the reclamation team doing?" Draif asked.

As soon as Finn was given the mission to find the Vextonians Wineon sold, he had put together a team of research investigators to locate as many of the Vextonians as possible. There were well over over two billion, so it was quite the job.

Once they had left Charybdis Station, Halli and her group had commandeered the conference rooms on the Blue Albatross and worked in shifts, day and night.

"With the help of Gus and some of the Charybdis Station techs planetside on Vextonar, we've finally recovered *all* of Wineon's records." Finn gave them a tight smile. "Property is chipped and tracked, so we have a lot to work with."

Fasi looked disgusted. "I know it's handy for us, but damn that makes me sick."

Finn whole heartedly agreed. "From Wineon's records, we have a complete list of all citizens sold and who they went to originally." He paused for a moment, not eager to pass on the latest news. "Earlier today, Halli and her team were able to confirm that around seventy-two thousand are dead. She used the information sent through their chips. I'll send you a list of their names and causes of death as soon as I can."

Fasi closed his eyes. "Gods, that is not what I wanted to hear."

"Slaves are the most vulnerable of the population." Draif's eyes were hard. "I take it many of the dead were the very old or the very young?"

Finn closed his eyes and nodded. "Halli and her team have started working their way through the lists of the living. As I wrote in my last report, we've recovered a good portion of them with the help of the media, our allies, and the yellow fleet in the Silverlight System. I'll send you an exact number tonight."

Fasi nodded sadly. "This is good news. Now, as you know, I'm concerned most about the missing Vextonians." Around two million of the Vextonians had been *gifted* to Teresa Malone, one of the leaders of Humans First. Halli had been unable to find any trace of them after they had been processed on Vextonar.

"We'll see what we can find on Rueal." Finn noticed he was stroking his tail and stopped. He was trying to break the nervous habit. "Hopefully, we can find them quickly."

Draif tapped his chin. "My contact, Aiden Crow, should be able to help. He'll meet you at the spaceport. You received my file on him?"

"Yep." Finn bit back a yawn. It had been a long day. "Former smuggler turned rebellion leader. Born and raised on Rueal. Hates Humans First." The file neglected to say why, and Finn had a feeling Draif had left a lot of Crow's personal info out.

At least he had included a picture. Finn hummed a moment, recalling the strong face, dark eyes, and broad shoulders of the hybrid. Aiden Crow was a fine-looking man.

"We also have some new information for you." Draif stared down at his tablet. "Gus was able to locate over a hundred unmarked transport ships that took a large number of Vextonians to Rueal. I'm sending the manifests to you now."

"Really?" Finn thanked the gods every day for the hacker Draif had persuaded to join Charybdis Station. Gus was a force to be reckoned with. "I'll have Halli compare it to our records. I'd bet you anything those are the missing Vextonians."

Hack scowled. "We suspect Malone auctioned them off on Rueal, but her warehouses are empty, and we can't find the documentation telling us who they were sold to."

"Can Gus access her files?" Finn asked.

"No." Draif's expression turned sour. "Right before she died, Malone managed to lock him out of her network. He hasn't been successful getting back in remotely."

"Can your contact help from her estate?" Finn had no clue what all it took to hack a network, but if Gus had someone on the ground, it had to be easier. Right?

Fasi shook his head. "Crow is having trouble getting back into her estate. Since her assassination, Malone's only remaining heir, her son, has reinforced security. He isn't joining the fighting, so there's that at least, but he's not exactly cooperating with the new government."

"Okay." Finn tapped his chin. "As soon as we get there, we meet up with Crow and infiltrate Malone's estate to search for information on the missing Vextonians."

"That's the plan." Hack looked troubled. "Most of the fighting is over. Rueal fell quickly, but there are still pockets of resistance. Humans First had a lot of powerful allies on the planet. Watch your back."

Fasi let out a deep sigh. "Cas's lieutenant is still there with the majority of his fleet, but most of the allies that joined us in taking the planet have left. I don't know how much backup you'll have, Finn."

"Should we send Cas back to Rueal?" Draif asked, head tilted and eyes full of consideration.

"No." Finn shook his head. "He needs to start helping the planets HF devastated. I can handle this. Halli and her team will keep sending locations out so we can retrieve the Vextonians, and I'll focus my search for Malone's group. I have my own small fleet and can call on the green fleet lieutenant if I need to." Finn knew Cas's lieutenant. Leslie was good at her job and wouldn't hesitate to help him if he needed it.

"You have Moyra too." Hack gave him a sly look. "How's that going for you?"

Finn's head fell back when he groaned, and he stared at the bridge's ceiling as they laughed at him. "She keeps shuttling over to train with me and steal my food. She's hits harder than Selene, but at least she doesn't eat as much as Fire."

Fasi gasped in mock outrage, hand pressed to his chest. "She hits harder than Selene?"

Hack chuckled. "Wait until I tell Selene. She'll take it as a challenge and kick your ass when you get back."

Finn whimpered and rubbed his ears, fingers stroking across the scar atop one of them. "No need for that."

Hack looked up from his communicator. "Too late. I already messaged her."

"I hate you." Finn glared and shook his head in disappointment.

Fasi chuckled. "We'll let you get back to work. Draif and Gus will keep you updated on any information that comes in. Let us know if you need anything."

"Will do." Finn glared at Hack until the screens went black.

"You know Selene is going to kick my ass too, don't you?" Moyra's voice came from beside Finn, making him jump. Her shield shimmered as she became visible.

Finn slowed his breathing, heartbeat gradually evening out. "Damn it, Moyra. You're not supposed to sneak around on my ship."

The human hybrid rolled her eyes and sprawled on one of the seats near Alluva. "Sneaking around is at least half the fun of being a covert operative. Don't steal my fun, lieutenant."

Alluva snickered, then pulled up her paused simulation, effectively ignoring them as she worked her way through a mine field.

Moyra eyed him. "This search is going to take forever. You know that, right? Months have passed, so there's no telling where Malone sent the Vextonians."

Finn sighed. "I know. It doesn't help that Gus can't hack her new system."

"How are we going to do this. Really?" Moyra made a face. "We can't just show up and depend on the smuggler."

Finn thought about the report on Aiden Crow. The man was interesting, that was for sure. Smugglers weren't exactly known for their caring nature, but Crow had readily joined the fight against HF, even when it didn't directly benefit him to do so. In fact, it could be argued the mess on Rueal was actually hurting Crow's business.

"We have a few resources." Finn tilted his head in thought. "We have a small fleet of our own and the Green fleet as backup. Plus, we have the Blue Albatross for transport and temporary housing of any Vextonians we recover." He smiled wryly. "We also have Wyther."

Moyra arched a brow. "The captain of the Blue Hope? What's so special about him?"

"He hates slavery." Finn leaned forward, eyes narrowing. "I mean, he *really* hates slavery. The man knows the inner workings of the slave market because he comes from a family of prominent slavers, and he will happily share that knowledge." *He'll also make a good point man.*

"Hmm. That's why you asked the Lord Admiral to have him join us." Moyra stood. "I think I'll go chat with Wyther. I feel as if I've neglected him."

Finn shuddered, feeling sorry for the man. "Don't hurt him too much, alright? The man gave up well deserved down time to help us out."

Moyra paused to scratch his ears. "You're such a fragile sweetie. A little pain does everyone some good."

Finn waited until she left, then stood. "I'm going to go to my office in case anymore calls come in."

"You got it, sir." Alluva grinned over her shoulder. "Lock the door behind you in case Moyra decides to come back."

"Very good point." Finn nodded and left the bridge.

The Blue Albatross had plenty of space and formidable defenses, but it was designed for people accustomed to luxury. The office suite next to the bridge was much larger than Finn needed, so he had adapted it to serve as his living space too. The outer room originally was designed as a reception area, but it made a nice-sized office space.

That left the captain's quarters available for Weber, the actual captain of the ship. Web's office was right across the hall, and Finn liked the convenience of their set up.

Finn pulled up the closest vid-screen and looked over the list Draif had sent him. A little over two million Vextonian citizens were listed by name, species, and next of kin. He immediately searched for two names and found them.

He smiled in satisfaction. *These are the missing Vextonians.*

He pulled a small brass medallion out of his pocket and ran it through his fingers for a moment before pulling up another screen. The picture at the top was of a young married couple with a toddler. The husband, Ival Topin, was human, and his wife was a Wello hybrid. Beneath the picture was a personal note from Ival: *My wife is Berenna and our son is Ezvin. They were taken in the night while I was at work. No one could trace them after they left Vextonar. Please find them.*

Finn rubbed his face and flattened his ears. A group of humans had left Vextonar and aided Hack and his fleet in destroying the Crellic Queen. Now, those humans were relying on Finn to find their lost loved ones. Some had already been located, but many hadn't.

"Lieutenant." Alluva's voice came from the wall comm. "Call coming through on your vid-screen from Charybdis Station."

"Thanks." Finn pocketed the medallion and dropped into the chair behind his desk to wait for the call to connect. He grinned when his best friend's face filled the screen. "Dannol, I thought you would be busy with Meggie and Nessa."

Dannol smiled wide, eyes soft and joyful. "Nessa is happy we're back, and Beck and the others are working on helping Meggie recover. We're having a movie night in a few minutes. I just wanted to check in on you before I got too distracted."

"Everything's nice and quiet." Finn pursed his lips. "Too quiet."

"Don't jinx yourself." Dannol gave him one of his dopey, happy looks. "Did General Hack talk to you yet about the Blue Fleet's operations?"

Finn leaned back, wary. "No. Why?"

Dannol practically bounced in place. "Once Hack started back to work, he noticed everything was better organized and running smoother than when he left. Hack about laid an egg."

Finn's eyes widened as he imagined Hack hatching an egg. "Would the chick look like Leti or Hack? Would it have feathers?"

Dannol snapped his fingers. "Focus, Finn. Everyone was super impressed. You know Hack got shit for promoting you to Blue Lieutenant."

Personally, Finn had thought his captain had lost his mind when he promoted him. Finn was a good communications officer, but lieutenant to a fleet was a big change. Well, he had thought it was a big change.

Finn shrugged. "I do the same thing I did when I was the communications officer on the Blue Solace. I keep everything organized and functioning, just on a bigger scale." He rubbed his ears. "I did get to lead an ambush and that was fun."

Dannol made a face. "You don't give yourself enough credit. Anyway, Hack will get around to thanking you." He looked to each side before leaning toward the screen. "I've heard that the Lord Admiral and Draif are busy picking up the pieces that nasty man Goel left behind. Cortez and Hald's industrial empires were already gobbled up by their competitors, but Goel's medical research and pharmaceutical companies are more complicated. I think the Lord Admiral is gonna try to help them figure things out."

Finn wrinkled his nose. "No wonder my call with them earlier was short and to the point. I don't envy them that mess."

Dannol nodded, then gave Finn a proud look. "I heard Hack tell Draif he was glad you were handling the missing Vextonians. He said he knows you'll handle every little detail."

Finn spun his chair around in a circle twice, then three times.

"Finn." Dannol tried for a stern voice, but the Havenite was incapable of being too harsh. He started giggling instead.

Finn stopped his chair and met his friend's kind gaze. "What if I don't find them all? What if they're lost forever?"

Dannol gave him a thoughtful look. "Would you ever stop looking for them?"

Finn's ears flattened, and he hissed. "Never. They were stolen away from their families, Dannol."

"Then they won't be lost forever." Dannol nodded, expression full of certainty. "Charybdis Station won't let them stay missing."

2

SUGARWORM SYSTEM, PLANET RUEAL

*A*iden Crow rode a speeder through the near empty street of Pagent's Distillery. The city was one of the last HF-controlled holdouts against the rebellion. The Jevio family had unofficially controlled the profitable city for generations, and they refused to give up that power.

As he turned into one of the darkened neighborhoods, Parker's voice came through the comm in Crow's helmet. "Michael Jevio just surrendered, boss." Crow's second-in-command was leading the attack at the Jevio mansion. "Old man Jevio isn't there, but we got the rest of the family."

"Good." Crow's voice was too gruff even to his own ears. "The government building just fell to Jada's soldiers."

"What went wrong?" Parker asked, voice solemn.

Damn asshole can read me too well. Crow zoomed through an empty shopping center, ignoring the burning garbage and bloodstained cement. "We lost more people than usual. City enforcement sided with Jevio's people, and the fucking Belcrest assassins showed up in force."

"Who did we lose?" Parker asked quietly.

"Horski and Mel." They had lost more, but those two had been Crow's people. Two people that Crow had dragged into this stinking pile of dog shit.

"Damn it," Parker cursed. The Dedril was quiet a moment. "Don't let this fuck with your head, boss. They knew what they were doing."

"Horski's wife wasn't so forgiving." Crow gritted his teeth as he drove past abandoned houses. He felt eyes watching him from the dark, and his gut churned in guilt. *Their city is torn apart.*

"You talked to her by yourself?" Parker cursed again. "Boss, that was stupid."

Crow drove past a familiar dilapidated office building. The security stations around the building were burning, smoke billowing from them. *Dad, you would hate to see it now. This place was your pride and joy.*

He shook his head and focused on the present. "I didn't want to wait. Mel's parents took it better. I'll make arrangements."

"I'll get Staci on it." Parker sighed. "Come home, boss. We'll drink to our friends."

"One more stop." Crow parked in front of a large, darkened house. The neighborhood had been an old and respected one before HF and the fighting. Now, it was almost as derelict as his dad's old office building.

"Tell your mom I said hello," Parker said wryly, then disconnected.

Crow powered down the speeder and climbed off. He removed his helmet and ran a hand over his short hair. It was cut almost to the scalp.

The house was a large two-story. Crow remembered many days spent in the lush backyard, reading in a hammock while his older brother built bird houses and other odds and ends.

After a moment he started up the cracked walk. Diana Crow's prized Rueal Sundrop bushes were now full of weeds and almost bare. The grass in the front yard was overgrown, but so were all the houses in the neighborhood. Pagent's Distillery's summers were wet and hot, so the grass would only get higher.

A curtain moved in the front window. *I remember when you'd run outside and greet me with a hug, Mom.*

He knocked on the door, then waited a good ten minutes for it to open.

"Aiden." His mom's eyes were empty and sunken. Her once vibrant, dark skin was dull and almost grey. Even the Wello spots that framed her face looked faded. "What are you doing here?"

"Can I come in?" Crow asked, feeling like he was a teenager again and arriving home late from a party.

She shrugged and opened the door. "Dermot came by and brought me groceries earlier."

Crow gave her a small smile. "I spoke with him yesterday. He and Jenise are going to move back here once things get settled. He'd like for you to stay with him, you know."

"I know what you two want," Diana said, grimacing. "I'm not leaving my house. Your father and I bought this place when we first moved to Pagent's Distillery, and I'll be damned if I leave it to burn."

Crow followed her into the kitchen. The house was dusty and dark. Dishes filled the sink and rotting fruit sat in a bowl on the counter. "You could come back, Mom."

"No. I've stayed out of the fighting, so people leave me alone here." She turned away from him and waved toward the table. "Sit down and I'll feed you. Right before you got here, they announced the city fell. I take it you were there fighting?"

"Yes, ma'am. I don't need any food."

"You'll eat what I make you. Tell me Jevio is dead."

"Not yet. Parker was leading the fighting at the Jevio estate. He told me Michael Jevio surrendered."

She slammed a loaf of bread on the table. "What about Philip Jevio? The fucking head of the Jevio family had my Perick murdered. He was stabbed at his desk, Aiden."

"I know, Mom." Crow rubbed his face. "He won't get away with it. HF is gone now, and the Jevio family is out of power. We'll find Philip."

"Perick built that company from the ground up." Diana keened quietly as she sliced a tomato. "It's all over now. Everything he did was for nothing."

Crow reached out and held her wrist. "He took care of us, Mom. You and Dad raised two good kids, and you know as well as I do that family was the most important thing to Dad. You still have Dermot and me."

She shook off his hand and finished making a sandwich before setting it in front of him. "Eat."

16

Crow sighed. "Yes, ma'am."

She sat in front of him. "What do you do now? There's what? A handful of cities left to take?"

"Three." Crow swallowed the dry lump of food and tried not to wince. His mom had been a good cook once.

"Then what?" She laughed bitterly. "Rueal's gone. Most of the non-humans were deported when Humans First took control, and now, they're gone too. What's left?"

Crow thought of the eyes that watched him from the darkened buildings and homes of the city. "There are more people still here than you think. We'll rebuild and make Rueal a better place for everyone."

Diana snorted. "Better men than you have tried before. Even if the Jevio family is ousted, someone just like them will take their place."

Crow set his sandwich down and leaned forward. "Not if we stand our ground and fight for something more. Mom, you know Dad would have –"

She slammed her hands on the table, making the plate jump. "Shut up! Perick had foolish ideas, and it got him killed."

Crow stood and paced around the kitchen. "Being a hybrid is what got him killed, Mom. His ideas weren't foolish. He wanted everyone to have a fair chance in this world and to be accepted for who they are."

"Doesn't matter now, does it?" she asked, sinking in on herself. "He's dead and I'm alone."

Crow tried to force his anger away. He knew people grieved differently. Crow wanted to fight and fix the problems that led to his dad's death. Dermot wanted to mourn and move forward with his own life and family. His mom... His mom wanted to give up.

"Why do you care anyway?" Diana asked, eyes hard. "You didn't want to be part of Perick's dreams of equality. Weren't you the one that told him Rueal would never change?"

Crow sank to his knees in front of her. His dad and him hadn't seen eye to eye on quite a few things. Rueal's potential was one of them. Perick Crow had worked to change the world around him by being a good person and treating others well. Aiden Crow was a smuggler who made a nice profit off the mistakes of large corporations.

Crow braced his hands on his knees and looked at the floor. "Yeah. I said that. I was wrong though. Look at what we accomplished, Mom."

Her laughter took him off guard, and he leaned back. Bitterness and pain made an awful sound when disguised as mirth.

"What you've accomplished?" Diana laughed harder. "All you've done is throw a tantrum because your daddy is dead. You get upset and help topple a government. What are you going to do now, Aiden? Fighting and killing is easy. How are you going to piece this world back together?"

He shifted on his knees and stood. "Jada is leading things. She'll do a good job running this place."

Diana leaned over the table, body shaking with laughter. "You're going to run, right? Help cause all this trouble, then run away to that ship of yours to fly around the system making money."

Crow threw his hands up. "What do you want, Mom?"

She looked up, laughter gone and face dead serious. "I want Philip Jevio's head on a fucking spike. I'm no better than you, son. I want my vengeance, and I don't give a damn about anything else."

"Mom, what kind of life is that?"

She snorted. "You're suddenly an expert on a good life? Kill old man Jevio and I'll be just fine." She waved a hand toward the door. "Go on now and be a good son."

"Mom." Crow reached out for her, but her hard glare stopped him.

"Go away, Aiden. I'm tired."

He closed his eyes for a moment, then turned to leave. "Yes, ma'am."

His speeder was gone when he left the house.

Parker sat in a personal shuttle, arm hanging out the window. "Hey, boss. Brisco loaded your speeder up and is taking it home."

Crow climbed in without a word. He didn't want to talk. He didn't want to think anymore. Parker pulled out, and Crow watched the desolate city speed by.

"I know this is your hometown, boss. It has to hurt to see it like this." Parker reached over and punched his arm. "You know this place looked like this before the fighting started, right? HF deported over a third of the population and thousands left of their own will after the city went to hell."

"I know." Crow settled his head against the window

as Parker pulled the shuttle up and into the air. Silence filled the vehicle, but it wasn't uncomfortable.

They flew away from the city and back toward home. Crow and his crew operated out of a rural, defunct vineyard. Crow had bought the place for cheap when the Rueal aristocrat's winery had gone under. The soil wasn't good for growing grapes, but it had a nice little landing pad and plenty of storage.

"Those Charybdis Station folks are getting here tomorrow." Parker's words broke the silence. "You meeting them at the spaceport?"

"Yeah. Seems like a good idea."

"How much help are we giving them?" Parker asked. "I'm all for finding missing people, but we have a lot on our table right now."

"They pulled together for us." Crow leaned back in his seat. "Without the green fleet and their allies, we wouldn't have stood a chance of removing HF from Rueal."

"Good point." Parker landed on the shuttle pad on top of Crow's house. His speeder was already in the covered ground parking spot. "Brisco got some intel on a small group of Vextonian slaves. Seems they were sold to the Quincey estate. We sent Joelle to check it out."

"Good to know." Crow let the warm familiarity of his home sink into his tired psyche.

The small villa was comfortable and serviceable. Crow may deal with luxury goods every day, but he wasn't a fan of them. His mom had always told him a house was made of *things*, but a home was made with a family. His crew was his family. Several houses were spread across the vineyard and each of his most trusted crewmembers had made a home there.

He leaned against the low wall of the shuttle pad and looked at the night sky. Both moons were bright against the black sky, and he could even see the green glow of the planet Tammol.

He looked away and down at the estate. *Fuck.* "I see Horski's house is empty already."

"Nadia isn't one to take her time." Parker leaned against the wall next to him. "She moves fast. Mel's parents will be by in a few days. Staci is making the arrangements for her funeral. Nadia didn't want our help with Horski. She didn't want his body. Nothing but the money you offered."

Crow leaned his head back and looked at the sky again. "I'm so tired of this. We got what we wanted, right?"

"Yep." Parker puffed his cheeks out, then slowly released his breath. "HF is decimated, Hald and Malone are dead, and the fighting is almost done. Now comes the hard part."

3

SUGARWORM SYSTEM, PLANET RUEAL

*F*inn watched through the viewport as they approached Rueal. The Green Fleet's presence was obvious. Their ships flew in and out of the six different spaceports, and one of Full Moon's ships was circling the planet as they helped repair the planetary defenses.

What was conspicuously missing were merchant vessels. Finn looked at Web. "Do you remember Leslie saying anything about an embargo or blockade?"

"Nope." The Drall shook his head and peered out the viewport. "To be honest, if the planet is in the kind of shape Leslie describes, then trade is the least of its worries."

Alluva and her copilot, Tobi, carefully maneuvered the Blue Albatross past the Green Fleet and through the planetary defenses. They landed in the Pagent's Distillery spaceport.

Finn smiled at Web as he took the captain's chair. "I'll just borrow this for a moment." He shot a look at the communications officer. "Ignali, pull up my captains."

A few moments later, the rest of his twelve captains watched him from various vid-screens.

"What are our orders, Blue Lieutenant?" As usual, Wyther was as formal as possible.

Over the past few years, Finn had adapted to being in charge of others, but he always felt a little nervousness when he stood in the spotlight. He pushed his butterflies away and focused.

He nodded to the screens. "We'll be spending some time on Rueal as we look for the missing group of Vextonians, but right now, we're light on information. It's early morning planetside, so I want each ship to take this time to refuel and restock. I'll meet with our contact and hopefully get more information. We'll meet at noon to discuss our plans going forward. Wyther, I want you and Moyra to meet our contact with me."

They signed off, and Finn headed for the cargo bay.

"How many soldiers do you want for security?" Web asked, following behind him.

Finn bit his lip and thought for a moment. "None with me but have everyone on call. I don't want to spook the smuggler, but I also don't want to be too trusting."

"You got it." Web nodded, then barked orders into his comm. He nudged Finn with his shoulder. "We're all eager to get out there and search. I swear the crew wants to comb the streets to find these people."

Finn rubbed his ears and his tail started twitching.

"We've all read the files on the missing Vextonians. It's hard to sit still while they're out there. We need to get the lay of the land and organize this search to be as efficient and effective as possible."

Web laughed loudly and thumped Finn's back with his big hand, making Finn stumble. "That's why you're the Blue Lieutenant. We'll be here if you need us."

Finn flushed but shot Web a grin. "Thanks."

Thirty minutes later, he stood with Moyra and Wyther at the center of the spaceport. There weren't a lot of people around, but he recognized Charybdis Station uniforms and a few other mercenary guild patches.

Wyther crossed his arms for the eightieth time and huffed out an irritated breath. "Should we go to the entrance? Maybe this contact is there?"

Finn groaned as he checked the time again. "No, this is where we were supposed to meet. Where the fuck is this guy?"

Moyra looked around and yawned. "Not here. Draif said he was reliable?"

"Yeah. He talked highly of *Mr. Aiden Crow.*" Finn's full bushy tail twitched in agitation. He wanted to get moving, damn it.

He sighed and looked out the window again. Pagent's Distillery's spaceport was the largest on Rueal, and it was in shambles around them. The once wealthy and pristine city looked like it had been stomped on. Most of the houses and businesses still stood, but all of large government and military buildings were just rubble.

"Looks rough, doesn't it?" Moyra moved to stand beside him. "It's easy to get caught up in our own losses and forget the impact HF had on the other worlds."

Finn's eyes watered, and he reached into his pocket to rub his fingers over the brass medallion. "Yeah. It's going to take years, maybe even generations, to fix what was broken."

Moyra said something, but Finn didn't hear her. He spun away from the window, ears perking up and nose twitching when he caught a whiff of the most tantalizing scent he'd ever smelled. It was like a mixture of sunshine and wildflowers with a bit of catnip to drive him crazy.

His eyes zeroed in on the large dark-skinned hybrid walking his way. *Mate!*

Moyra waved a hand in front of his face. "Hello. Is anyone home?"

He hissed and pushed her hand out of his way. "Don't block my view. Catnip and sunshine, isn't he beautiful? His smell, Moyra. Oh gods, I could roll in it."

Wyther half smiled. "Oh, dear."

Moyra arched a brow. "You sound like a gramma, Wyther."

The large Drall gave her a dry look. "You make me feel like a gramma, Moyra."

Crow, the stunning example of pure perfection, stopped in front of him. Two people stood behind him, but they were completely and utterly unimportant. Crow nodded at them and eyed Finn. "Blue Lieutenant Sterling?"

Finn didn't recall moving. He was beside Moyra

and Wyther one moment, and the next he was draped over the lovely hybrid's shoulder and snuggling into his side. "Hi, my name is Finn. You have the most beautiful eyes I've ever seen. They're brown with little flecks of... is that green? Yeah, that's green."

"Are you wearing catnip perfume or something?" Moyra eyed the stranger. "Usually, he only acts this ridiculous when he's had a little too much catnip."

The two men behind Crow watched them in fascination, but Finn couldn't seem to focus on anything but his mate's eyes. "It's like your eyes are hypnotizing pools of glitter."

Moyra snorted. "Oh fuck, I need to record this."

"I got it covered," one of the strangers said, holding up his communicator. "I'll send it to you later."

Crow winced and tried to shrug Finn off his broad, muscular shoulder. Finn squeezed his arm. Yep. Broad and muscular. Finn clung on, digging his tiny claws into the man's thick jacket.

The man winced and gave up trying to move away. "I'm Aiden Crow. We have things to deal with, right? We can talk about whatever this is later."

Finn sighed and hugged his arm. "It's called mating, but you're right. We have some Vextonians to find."

Crow looked uneasy. "Are you, uh, going to let go of my arm?"

Finn blinked. Was the man serious? "No," he answered, drawing out the word. *Silly mate.* "Now, to start, the Lord Admiral wanted me to tell you he appreciates any help you can give us and will be more than happy to pay you and your people for your time."

Crow's eyes narrowed as he tried to pull his arm free. "That won't be necessary."

Finn shrugged. "Okay. Do you have any intel for us at the moment? I have a few ideas of where to look, but you know your planet."

Crow shuffled his feet and sighed before nodding to the giggling woman behind him. "Joelle here followed some rumors last night and found a small group of the Vextonians at an estate near here. An old Rueal aristocratic family named Quincey owns it."

Joelle's expression sobered. "There're forty-two Vextonians among their other slaves."

"Can you tell us anything about their security?" Finn asked, leaning his head against Crow's arm.

Joelle nodded. "Sure can."

"Moyra, will you take Joelle to the Blue Albatross to conference with her?" Finn noticed Wyther's frown. "Pull Wyther and his crew in if you need them."

Wyther brightened. "Are we taking all the slaves or just the Vextonians?"

Finn frowned. "Technically, slavery is legal on Rueal. However, Charybdis Station publicly announced, several times, that anyone who purchased one of the Vextonian citizens and didn't immediately hand them over would be considered an HF sympathizer."

The man that had come with Crow looked up from his communicator. "Jada made that announcement all over Rueal the past few weeks."

"We *could* do this the nice way." Finn tilted his head,

ears twitching. "We could request they turn over the Vextonians."

Moyra and Wyther shared a wicked look.

"Now, where's the fun in that?" Moyra asked.

Finn nodded. "Get a peek at their security. We need to move fast and minimize casualties as much as possible. However, if the Quincey family is HF, or even HF supporters, they're the enemy."

Joelle looked uncertain. "Their security is pretty formidable."

Moyra wrapped an arm around Joelle's shoulders. "That just makes it more fun. Come on back to Finn's big, fancy ship and tell us all about it."

Finn watched Moyra, Wyther, and Joelle walk away before turning his attention back to Crow. "Can I call you Aiden?"

Crow rubbed the center of his brow. "Can I stop you?"

"Nope."

"Then, please, call me Aiden."

"Thank you, Aiden. Do you have any more intel for us?"

"That's all for now." Crow frowned. "I suspect there's something for us on Malone's estate, but we haven't been able to get in."

The other man winced. "Malone's heir is her youngest son, Verulo Malone. He's a dipshit if ever I met one, and he's scared to death. The man has more security on that estate than the government buildings of Pagent's Distillery did before we took it."

"Getting in there is our next logical step, and the

sooner the better." Finn rubbed his chin back and forth on Crow's arm. "Come aboard and we'll talk more. We should have had this conversation on the ship anyway. I *may* be a little out of it." He breathed in Crow's scent. "You smell delicious, Aiden."

The stranger barked out a laugh, then grinned at Finn. "I'm Parker, by the way. I imagine we'll get to know one another." Crow growled under his breath, and Parker's eyes widened. "Well, we won't get to know each other *that* well. Calm down, boss."

Macho mate. Finn hid a smile and tugged his mate toward the Blue Albatross. "I have a wonderful office. You'll like it."

Crow grunted.

"You're a man of many words, I see." Finn leaned his head back against Crow's arm as they walked. "I know this is poor timing, Aiden. I'll try to rein things in soon so we can focus on the mission. It's just that I've looked forward to meeting my mate for a long time."

Parker fell several steps behind them to provide Finn and Crow with some privacy, and Finn decided he really liked the man.

Crow grunted again. "We don't have time to mate. There's too much to do. Maybe in a few years –"

"Hah," Finn forced out between his gritted teeth. "That's not happening, Aiden. I'll take things a little slow, but I'm not waiting years for my mate. Now, if you don't want me, that's different."

Crow was quiet for a few moments, then unclenched his jaw. "I should tell you I don't want you."

"But you can't." Finn tilted his face and gently bit

Crow's arm. "Don't be an asshole. Fate or whatever deity you believe in is telling us that we belong together. However, I understand that we just met, and we don't know each other. In time, we'll figure things out, but we need to be together to do that."

Crow's expression looked decidedly sour, and Finn tried not to take it personally. He had always thought his mate would be as happy and excited as him when they met. Leti and Hack had fallen for each other quickly, as had several of the other couples of the Blue Solace crew. His mate looked like he'd swallowed a bug.

Finn pushed his hurt away and leaned his head back against Crow's arm. "First, though, we focus on the Vextonians."

4

$\mathcal{C}$row tried to ignore the warm weight curled into his side as they walked down the wide hallways of the large ship. It was hard to do when his dick was telling him he *really* needed to pay attention to the Cardinal beside him. *I don't have time for a mate.* Not even an adorably snuggly one.

Finn Sterling was a sight to behold. The Cardinal's hair was black, and his ears and tail matched perfectly, both a little on the bushy side. The man's eyes, though, were what kept Crow's attention. His golden feline eyes seemed to look straight through Crow. It was both compelling and disturbing.

I really don't have time for a mate, he reminded himself for the hundredth time since meeting Finn.

"Here's my office."

Finn's voice startled Crow from his dazed state. The room was already full of people and practically thrummed with excitement. Ten uniformed people sprawled around the room, relaxing in chairs and on sofas.

"These are the rest of my captains. Weber, Althea, Gryllen, Ronnie, Vanich, Dhami, Cardozo, Qural, Bryant, and Chambers." Finn introduced him to the captains, then settled him into the chair behind the desk.

Crow shifted to get comfortable and cleared his throat. "Okay, so Malone's estate."

Finn sat in his lap.

Almost as one, the captains' eyes widened.

"Uh, Lieutenant?" Captain Weber asked. "Is there something you want to tell us?"

Parker snickered from the door. "These two lovebirds are mates. Here, I'll send you a video."

Finn settled his back into the curve of Crow's arm. "Wyther and Moyra are working together to liberate a small group of the missing Vextonians, but at this moment, we have no information leading to the others." He turned those damn golden eyes on Crow. "We need onto Malone's estate."

Crow's brain stopped working. Fortunately, Parker seemed to still be functioning.

"The security for the estate is insane," Crow's friend said. "The estate itself is the size of a small town, and Verulo Malone's private security patrols it at all times."

"Any sign of mercenaries or the Belcrest assassins?" Finn asked, head tilted to the side in curiosity.

Crow's voice was too deep and rough, but at least he could answer the question. "Not that we can see, but we can't get very close."

"We have personal shields that can help with that." Finn bit his lip, eyes narrowed in thought. "I'm thinking we sneak in and see what we can find. Two teams go in. One to determine weaknesses within Verulo's security, and the second to look for any information we can find on the missing Vextonians. I'm betting Halli or one of her techs can help us with any virtual security they have."

"Who goes?" Althea, one of the captains, asked.

"Weber will lead the team to analyze the security." Finn wiggled his brows at Parker. "Are you okay to go with him? We'll share some of our tech with you. I promise you'll like it."

Parker grinned. "Now, how can I turn that down?"

Finn nodded, then turned his attention to a small Havenite woman leaning against the wall. "Ronnie, you'll lead the second team. I'll ask Halli for one of her techs to help with Malone's network."

Ronnie grinned "Perfect."

"I'll accompany you," Finn added.

The smile fell from her face, and the captains exchanged worried looks. Crow wasn't exactly pleased with the idea either. *Too dangerous.*

"Lieutenant, are you sure that's a good idea?" Weber asked.

"We need you leading and delegating," Althea added.

Finn's rumbling growl quieted the mutters in the room. "I understand your concern, and I certainly won't be charging into every single battle and skirmish we end up in, but I *need* to get a feel for Verulo Malone.

Right now, he is what's standing between us and the information we need. If we fuck this up by choosing the wrong path, we lose more than time."

Althea sighed but nodded in agreement. "Sorry, Lieutenant."

Finn wiggled farther into Crow's arms. "No problem. Now, I need to talk with Gus, and we can plan the mission. If possible, we'll go tonight. I don't want to give them any warning, and once we start moving, news will spread fast and that gives people time to scatter."

Crow sighed. Someone would have to watch Finn's back, and he didn't like the idea of his mate going into this kind of situation without him. "I'll go with you tonight."

Finn's eyes grew all shimmery, and Crow forced himself not to melt into a useless pile of moldable putty.

"This will be our first date," Finn whispered, then bit his lip. "You won't even be able to see what I wear. Damn it. At least we can hold hands."

Weber buried his face in his hands and shook with laughter. "I can't wait to tell General Hackett about this."

Finn sniffed and eyed his captains. "Alright, everyone out. Weber and Ronnie, you two be back here in an hour to plan. I'll talk to Gus and get his advice for the network security." He gave Crow a soft look. "You can stay, Aiden."

Crow arched a brow. "Would you actually let me leave?"

Finn shook his head and patted Crow's cheek. "No."

———

AFTER SEVERAL HOURS OF BEING FINN'S CHAIR, IT FELT nice to stand, even if it was behind a tree a mile away from the Malone estate. *Yeah, you just hated having your mate on your lap all day.* Crow told his inner self to shut up.

Finn clipped a small personal shield to Crow's belt. "This shield hides you completely. Don't ask me how it works. Beck tried to explain it to me once, but it just gave me a headache."

Crow was a little skeptical. "Sure, okay. What about that bot circling your head? I've never seen one like that." Several of the Charybdis Station soldiers gathering with them had one or two bots circling them.

Finn looked up and grinned. "Beck made them for us." He tapped the webbed device sticking to the side of his face. "This is a neuro-something-or-other. It links me to my bot. I named him Rufus."

Crow blinked a few times, then stared at the bot. *Rufus.*

"Rufus has a combination of phasers in him." Finn tapped a vibroblade strapped to his back. "I'm a lot better with my blade than a phaser, so Rufus backs me up."

"Rufus." Crow nodded. "Okay."

Parker exchanged an amused look with him. "Your bot seems nice, Finn."

Finn snickered. "You two will want one of your

own soon enough." He turned to Ronnie, Weber, and the soldiers. "Okay. Single file and shields up. Keep a hold on the person in front of you until you get to the estate. Then, do your part and retreat back here. Medics are with the shuttles and backup is available if things go wrong. Any questions?"

"No, sir!"

Finn nodded. "Let's do this."

Crow's mate and the other Charybdis Station soldiers activated their shields and disappeared along with their bots.

"What the fuck?" Parker reached out and poked the space where Finn had stood.

"Stop poking me." Finn's voice made Crow jump. "I *told* you what the shields did. Now shield up. We need to move."

Crow winced and did as he was told, then told his heart to stop racing when Finn took his hand. "I'm ready."

"Good." Finn sounded amused.

They covered the mile quickly and in complete silence. It was eerie as hell, but not as strange as when they all simply walked past each of the patrols. *Damn, I'm keeping this shield.*

Malone's estate was a striking contrast to the abandoned homes and crumbling government buildings of Pagent's Distillery. The sprawling villa with its perfectly landscaped grounds and tranquil atmosphere made him want to punch someone. Teresa Malone and her two eldest children may be dead, but her remaining family didn't seem to be hurting too badly.

Finn led him slowly through the servant's halls, pausing to listen to hurried conversations between Malone's slaves.

"He's an overgrown child," a woman whispered to another slave. She balanced a load of laundry on her hip. "I've made his bed six times this morning, but he said I didn't *do it right*. What the hell?"

"At least you're not one of his toys," the other slave said, shuddering. "I feel so sorry for that little hybrid."

The woman's eyes grew sad. "She keeps crying for her mate."

Finn's hand tightened in his. Crow had a feeling something had just pissed his mate off.

The other slave shook himself. "I hate it here so much, but it's all I've ever known. Imagine being free, then forced into this."

"Please don't be alarmed." Finn's voice startled both of the slaves and Crow.

"Who's there?" The man looked around, eyes wild.

Interestingly enough, the woman's eyes widened, and she smiled. "Are you that nice assassin that killed Mistress Teresa? Lodea said he was very polite when she came into the office right after he killed the mistress."

"Nice assassin?" Crow snorted. "I've never heard an assassin called nice before."

"You've clearly never been Teresa Malone's slave," the woman said, eyes hard.

"Sandve was the assassin," Finn said. Crow could

hear the smile in Finn's voice and had the sudden urge to murder Sandve. Finn sounded *fond* of the stupid assassin.

"Did he send you?" The woman again looked hopeful. "Master Verulo isn't as bad as the others were, but he's still an asshole."

"Donna," the male slave hissed and looked around again. "What if they're lying and you just insulted our master?"

"My name is Finn, and I'm with Charybdis Station. This is my –"

"Associate," Crow hurried to interject.

"Mate. He's my mate." Finn sounded smug. "This is our first date."

"This is an unusual date." Donna grinned.

Crow sighed. "He's an unusual man."

"Anyway." Finn cleared his throat. "We're here looking for a large number of Vextonian citizens that were sold into slavery and transported to Rueal by Teresa Malone."

Donna nodded. "It was all kind of a big deal here. Most were kept in her warehouses in town, but several of the more exotic and attractive hybrids were brought here before moving on."

"Where did they move on too?" Crow asked.

The woman shrugged, but the man looked uneasy.

"Sir?" Crow prompted him.

The man flushed. "No one calls me *sir*." He shook his head. "I'm Master Verulo's attending slave when he's here on the estate. I've heard things about that group of slaves."

"Bertie, you never said anything." Donna pouted. "I tell you everything."

"It's strange." Bertie looked around again before staring at Donna. It took a minute for Crow to realize he was talking toward her in case they were being watched. "Master Verulo was angry because they were marked to go somewhere else. He whined and complained to his mother, and eventually she gave him his current favorite bedslave. The others were sent to someone else. Someone Master Verulo absolutely despises."

"Do you have a name?" Finn asked.

Bertie swallowed hard. "I heard it a few times from Master Verulo. He called him the Weasel."

Crow cursed under his breath. "That isn't good."

"Who is he?" Finn asked and squeezed his hand.

"A fucking pirate." Crow rubbed between his eyes. *The fucking Weasel.*

Donna made a face. "He calls himself the Weasel? That seems kind of stupid."

Finn snickered. "I guess we need an owl or something. What eats weasels?"

"He's a fucking nightmare." Crow groaned. "He's a big pain in the ass that preys on merchant ships. The dickass has a fleet and a base somewhere in the system."

"Okay, so a group of the Vextonians went to him." Finn was quiet for a moment. "The others were kept at the warehouses and likely sold from there."

"That's what we know." Donna paused. "Are you going to get them?"

"Yes." Finn's voice sent a shiver down Crow's back. His mate was too cute to sound so vicious.

"What about Master Verulo's bedslave?" Bertie asked. "Can you help her?"

"We'll take the estate tomorrow evening." Finn growled, voice deepening. "Verulo Malone kept a Vextonian slave after being ordered to hand any he had over. That makes him an enemy and gives us a reason to take him out."

"What about us?" Donna asked.

"Try to keep any slaves or servants out of the barracks during the attack, and keep your heads down. Afterward, you're spoils of war, and Charybdis Station doesn't deal in slavery, so you'll be freed." Finn tugged Crow's hand. "We need to finish looking around. Thank you for your help."

Donna and Bertie stared at each other in amazement.

"We'll be free?" Bertie asked.

"Yes." Finn pulled him down the hall. "See you tomorrow."

They spent a solid two hours eavesdropping on the servants and security guards but learned nothing more about the Vextonians. Crow hoped Ronnie and her group had more luck in Verulo's office and private rooms.

They left the estate and walked back to the meeting place, hand in hand. Crow liked the warmth of his mate's fingers in his.

"Charybdis Station really hates slavery, huh?" he

asked. He had never liked the institution, but so many worlds across the galaxy dealt in it.

"Our Lord Admiral and the other leaders in the Anchor's Rest System declared our system a safe haven." Finn sounded almost wistful. "It was a huge deal at the time. I think I was ten or so."

"A few of the planets in our system abolished it." Crow let himself relax, perversely happy his mate couldn't see him, so he didn't have to keep up the gruff persona. "Tammol did early on about a hundred years ago, but Aruta did away with it too about five years ago. My dad threw a party to celebrate."

"Really?" Finn sounded delighted.

"Yeah. He had ideas about equality, and slavery didn't fit well with them." Crow smiled softly. "Dad and me only agreed on a few things, but one of them was slavery. He hated that I smuggled goods in and out of Rueal, but when it came to slaves, he was more than happy to have me sneak them off planet."

"You and your dad did that?" Finn squeezed his hand. "That is... I don't know what to say. I'm glad you're my mate. Do I get to meet him?"

Crow could almost feel the peace drain from his body and mind. "He died. I'm surprised Draif didn't tell you."

"I'm sorry, Aiden." Finn pulled him to a stop, and Crow soon had an armful of mate. "Draif kept your file bare of personal details. He can keep a confidence."

Crow propped his chin on Finn's head. "I guess he can. My dad was killed by a prominent family in Pagent's Distillery. He was the CEO of a large production company. Teresa Malone and the Jevio family worked together to have my dad murdered, then put a human in his place. Dad built that company himself, and the board just handed it over to HF."

"Malone is dead."

"Yeah. Philip Jevio isn't. Not yet." Crow let Finn go and started moving again.

They arrived back at the shuttle shortly after. Finn deactivated his shield, and Crow did the same, a little awed at their sudden appearance.

Finn leaned up on his tiptoes and pressed his lips to Crow's in a soft, sweet kiss. "This was a really good first date. We had some fun and are getting to know one another. I can't wait for our next one."

Crow snorted and pulled Finn into his arms. He cupped the back of the Cardinal's head and held him still as his mouth took Finn's in a hard, deep kiss. Crow let himself get lost in the taste of his mate. He didn't know Finn, not really, but everything about the man drew him in and turned him into a ball of want.

Finn melted against him, arms wrapping around Crow's waist as he tried to climb him. Crow could feel his mate's hard dick pressed against his thigh.

"Well, well, well." Parker appeared beside them as his shield deactivated. "What do we have here?"

Finn leaned back and glared at Crow's friend. "It's called a kiss. Shut up and let me enjoy it."

Crow grinned and set Finn back on his feet. The rest of the two teams were appearing around them, all watching Finn and Crow in amusement.

"Really, Lieutenant." Weber shook his head in

disappointment. "Groping your mate in the woods like a teenager."

"There was a perfectly good shuttle right there." Ronnie waved toward the shuttles. "Have some class."

Crow rubbed his chin over Finn's head. "It really was a good first date."

---

5

*F*inn had barely gotten into his bedroom when his comm chimed. Ignali's voice was a little too chirpy for this late in the evening. "Call coming in from Charybdis Station, Lieutenant."

He scowled and rubbed his ears. "I'll take it in my room. Thanks, Ignali."

His vid-screen activated and several grinning faces filled his view. Dannol sat directly in front of the screen, and Hack, Leti, and Finn's other friends piled behind him.

Dannol practically bounced in his seat. "Weber sent us an interesting video."

Finn tried for an overdramatic, fake yawn. "Oh dear, look at the time. I think I need to go to bed."

"You met your mate, Finn!" Leti clapped happily. "It was so cute too. You got all flustered and handsy."

"Don't tease him, baby." Hack wrapped an arm around Leti's shoulders. "Not everyone can be as calm and collected as we were when we met."

Draif snorted. "Does anyone here remember them being calm and collected?"

"Nope."

"Fuck, no."

"Are you kidding?"

"It was disturbingly sweet," Selene said, voice monotone as usual. The Siren's expression was bland as she stared at Finn. "Your mate looked unhappy."

Finn groaned and fell into a chair. "I'm working on it. We had our first date."

Hack winced. "Web told me. Uh, you know a reconnaissance mission isn't really a good date, right?"

Leti elbowed Hack in the side. "Don't listen to him, Finn. It sounds like it went well. Web had pictures of your kiss, and whoa, that was hot." He closed his eyes and fanned his face.

Finn grinned and propped his chin on his fist. "It was a really nice kiss."

Hack shook his head. "What did you guys find out?"

"There are some slaves still on Rueal." Finn scowled. "Halli went with Ronnie and was able to hack Malone's newest network. Despite all the media coverage and many warnings, the aristocratic families here haven't handed over the Vextonians they purchased. I'm kind of happy because this means we get to free *all* their slaves instead of just the Vextonians."

"Send them here if they want to come." Leti's face was set with determination. "I'll find them a home and a position."

Hack leaned in to kiss Leti's head. "Tammol and

Genarg have also offered homes for anyone, freed slave or not."

"We'll let them all know." Finn bit his lip. "We also discovered three large groups were sent off planet. One to Dramacus, another to one of Rueal's moons, and one final group seemingly just disappeared. They're nowhere in Malone's system, but we think that last group went to a pirate named the Weasel."

"The Weasel?" Dannol snickered.

"I know, right?" Finn chuckled before shaking his head. "We'll get the ones here on Rueal tomorrow evening. I want it to be a concentrated attack so we keep surprise on our side."

"Good plan." Hack's smile was smug. "I *told* Sheria you were the right man for the job. She wanted to send her lieutenant."

Leti rolled his eyes. "You're ridiculous, Will."

"We'll let you get some sleep now. You have a busy day tomorrow." Dannol tapped the screen. "I miss you, fuzz butt. Be careful, okay?"

"Miss you too." Finn stared at the screen long after it had gone black. He really did miss Dannol and the others.

A call came from Dannol's vid-screen again. Finn frowned and answered it. "Forget something?"

Fire was the only one there. His face was too close to the screen and Finn could almost see up his nose. It took a moment, but Finn noticed the tear tracks on Fire's cheek. "Fire, what's wrong?"

Fire's lip trembled. "I wanted to be the one to tell you. Last night, Marshmallow passed away."

Finn gave his friend a sympathetic look. "I'm sorry, Fire. I know how much you love your guinea pigs."

"Jellybean and I are devastated." Fire wiped his eyes. "Sebby said guinea pigs don't live very long, but they live full lives to make up for it. Marshmallow had a good, full life. It was just her time. I'm worried about Jellybean now."

"All you can do is make sure Jellybean has the best guinea pig life he can."

Fire swallowed hard, then nodded. "Death said that sometimes we lose our friends, but they'll always be with us in our memories."

Finn's own eyes grew wet and he took the medallion from his pocket and rubbed his thumb over the portrait on one side. "He's right."

Fire nodded. "Anyway, I think Marshmallow would want you to have her favorite bell. I'm gonna leave it at your house, okay?"

Finn gave him a soft smile. "Thank you, Fire. I'm honored."

Fire's lip trembled again and he turned away, ending the call.

"Poor Fire." Finn looked around his rooms, heart suddenly heavy. His bed was a comfortable mess of blankets and pillows, and his black aerial silks draped dramatically from the high ceiling. He had comfortable furniture to nap in and a big vid-screen to watch. Finn didn't lack in comfort or friends, but something was missing.

He peeled his clothes off and put them in the laundry chute before taking a quick shower. He dried off and jumped in the middle of his bed, then hugged one of his larger pillows to him. He would never admit it aloud, but he envied Leti all his children and pets. His friend was *never* alone.

To some that might sound like a nightmare, but Finn had spent most of his life alone. He knew what lonely felt like, and now that he had spent most of the day at Aiden's side, Finn knew he would never feel complete again without him. *I need my mate.*

———

THE NEXT EVENING, FINN DRESSED WITH CARE. He donned his most flattering lacy underwear and admired his sturdy frame in the mirror of the bathroom. He was short, but his time on the silks had given him some muscles. His belly, however, was a little too soft and showed his love of food.

"I look good," he told his reflection, turning around and admiring his muscled butt. His dark green briefs were lace vines with tiny red lace roses. He almost hated to don his uniform, but one couldn't go into battle in one's underwear. Well, that's what Selene had told him years ago during training.

Finn clipped a few extra shields on his belt and grabbed his favorite phasers. Selene had gifted them to him when he passed his first round of training when he was nineteen.

"Should we bring Beck's fancy grenades, Rufus? Aiden might like them." Finn watched his bot lift from its shelf and start circling his head. "I know, I know.

Better safe than sorry. I'll bring them. Oh, I should put my jumpy boots on, shouldn't I?"

He slid his feet into the sturdy black boots and fastened the sides. He felt it link through the flexible metal headpiece he wore. "I love Beck's toys, Rufus."

His bot didn't answer him.

"Maybe I should see about adopting one of the Fyrelings." Finn shook his head. "Then, I wouldn't just be talking to myself."

His comm chimed, and Ignali's voice filtered through his headpiece. "Lieutenant, everyone's ready."

"Is he there?" Finn didn't even try to hide his excitement.

Ignali laughed. "Yes, sir. Your man is all dressed in black and looking damn good."

A purr rumbled in his chest. "Thanks."

He quickly made his way to the launch room. The Blue Albatross was a functional battlecruiser and could easily hold hundreds of soldiers. Right now, most of his fleet gathered together.

Finn's gaze went straight to Aiden. His mate stood with several other strangers dressed in plain body armor.

Finn smiled softly and waved. *He brought his crew to help. How sweet.*

Weber cleared his throat and nudged him. "Lieutenant?"

Finn huffed. "I'm coming."

Weber laughed at him, and Finn finished walking to the slightly raised staircase. All of his captains gathered with him.

He looked out over the soldiers. "Alright, everyone. Tonight, we make our first move to free the Vextonians President Wineon gave to Teresa Malone."

The group cheered, and Finn grinned. They were all eager to help.

"Aiden Crow and his team found a group of forty-two of the Vextonians on the Quincey estate near here. Moyra will lead her team to take the estate and free all slaves there. Last night, we discovered several other groups were being held here on Rueal. The largest one is at a rural estate belonging to the Jevio family. Wyther, Althea, and a regiment of Rueal's military will take it."

"How many were there?" one of Ronnie's soldiers asked.

"One hundred and sixteen," Finn answered. "The other groups are on smaller estates and are assigned to smaller forces. You all know your assignments. In this case, any slaves you find that are owned by those with the Vextonians are now ours. Bring them here so we can free them."

Weber waited until the cheering ended to step up beside him. "Are you sure I can't talk you out of going after Malone's estate? We got the information we needed, and it's just one Vextonian. We might be able to sneak her out."

Finn shook his head. "I made a promise. There are other slaves there."

Weber gave him a sad look. "Ending slavery on Rueal isn't our mission, Finn."

"You and each of the other captains have everything

handled. Ignali and Alluva will kept us all in contact." Finn patted his shoulder. "I have a good group going with me."

Weber sighed. "There's no use protesting. Here comes your mate, and it looks like he brought his friends."

Finn went straight into Crow's arms. "Hi. Did you get all your business work stuff done this morning?" That was the excuse Crow had given for not coming straight to Finn this morning, but Finn didn't buy it. Crow had looked too sad for it to just be work.

Crow nuzzled behind Finn's ear. "Okay, so I had to go to some funerals. We lost two of our people in the attack on Pagent's Distillery."

Finn pinched Crow's side, and his mate yelped. "Why didn't you say that? I would have been there for you."

Crow's eyes softened. "You would have, wouldn't you? I'm not use to having someone of my own, Finn. Please be patient."

"I can be patient." Finn reached out and covered Moyra's mouth when she started to laugh. "At least you aren't still wanting me to wait a few years to date you." A wet tongue licked his hand. "Eww, Moyra!"

She grinned and sauntered past them. "Excuse me, folks. I have Vextonians to rescue."

Finn rolled his eyes, then took a minute to talk to each captain before they left. Soon enough, Finn and Crow's group were the only people left in the launch room.

He waved his hand to get their attention. "Alright,

as we talked about last night, each of you have three jobs for phase one of this mission. First, sneak onto the estate. Second, lay your trap or sabotage your assigned target. Third, get the hell out of the estate. Once each person is back outside with the rest of the group, we'll time it all right, hopefully, and set everything off. After that, it's going to be chaos. Take out as much of their security as you can and stay alive. Remember, if the fighting gets hectic, activate visibility. No one needs to get shot by accident."

Finn led Crow to his shuttle. "Your people are okay with helping us?"

"Yeah. They want to help." Crow opened the door and helped Finn into the shuttle. "Is this our second date?"

Finn smiled and leaned his head against Crow's shoulder. "Yes, it is."

Parker laughed from the front of the shuttle. "You two are kinda strange."

Finn propped his chin on Crow's shoulder and watched his mate smile. "We're a good strange."

"What did you do today?" Crow asked.

Finn walked his fingers down Crow's arm, then gripped his hand. "Planning and training. We scouted all of the smaller estates and got the medical bays ready. Halli found more locations for the other Vextonians, and I correlated pickups for them."

Crow shook his head, looking a little awed. "That's a lot of work for one day. How many of the others have you found?"

"All together, over a billion."

Parker whistled from the front. "Whoa. That's a lot of people."

"Wineon sold over half of Vextonar's population." Finn fought back a snarl. "Vextonar's a small planet, population around four billion. We have a lot of people to find, and we *will* find them."

"How many are we rescuing today?" Crow's friend Brisco asked.

Finn made a face. "Only six hundred and fifty-eight. That's barely a dent in the amount of Vextonians Malone was given."

"How many are there?" Crow asked.

"Two million seventy-five thousand three hundred and twenty-two."

Crow winced. "I would say I'm surprised, but Malone ran easily twice that many slaves through her warehouses before she was killed. She had only starting dipping into the slave trade, but she had a firm grip on the market in this system."

"Before HF, I'd find it hard to believe a planet leader could sell off its own people." Brisco sounded disgusted. "If they would have thought of it, I bet the former president of Rueal would have done exactly what Wineon did instead of deporting so many people."

A growl built in Finn's chest. "I hope they find Wineon wherever she's hiding. I can't wait to see her pay for her actions."

Parker and Brisco started a conversation with the rest of Crow's people, and Crow leaned into him and spoke quietly. "You remind me a little of my dad."

Finn tilted his head. "In what ways?"

Crow propped his head back against the seat. "Dad had principles. When he saw injustice, it made him mad. He wanted to help everyone."

Finn swallowed. "That's... That's a really nice thing to say, Aiden." He had to blink away tears. *What the hell is wrong with me?*

"He and I would fight about stuff all the time." Crow swallowed. "I could ignore things. If I didn't want to deal with the drama, I could just look away. Dad couldn't." The bitterness in Crow's laugh hurt Finn's heart. "He was a better man than me."

Finn was quiet for a moment. "I don't know the right thing to say, Aiden. Your dad sounds like he was a really good guy, but you can't be him. No matter how hard you try. You can only be you."

Crow gave him a half-hearted smile. "What if you don't like the person I am?"

Finn narrowed his eyes. "That goes both ways. What if you don't like me?"

"I find it hard to believe I won't." Crow pressed a soft kiss on his hand.

"Then you know how I feel." Finn tried to keep his anger out of his voice. "The man I see right here is a pretty damn good catch. You've led the fight to push HF from Rueal and you've helped us gather information. That doesn't sound like a man who doesn't care about others."

Crow looked out the window. "Maybe you're right. Sometimes I don't know who I really am."

You aren't the only one, handsome. Finn pinched the

skin on Crow's wrist and he looked back at him. "Figure that shit out. Selene told me you can't fall in love with someone if you don't love yourself first. I don't know if I believe her, but she's pretty smart."

Crow smirked. "Draif says Selene is a force all her own. If she said it, it must be true. I guess growing up on Charybdis Station was nice, huh?"

Finn shrugged, nerves building in his stomach. "I didn't go to Charybdis Station until I was seventeen. I grew up on Cardinal's Hold."

"Oh, I'm sorry. I just assumed you had. Is your family on Charybdis Station too?"

Finn ignored his question and stood when the shuttle stopped. "Looks like we're here, so we better get moving."

Crow pulled him back down and into his lap. "Finn? We'll come back to this conversation."

Finn tried to keep his face clear of emotion. "We have people waiting on us."

Crow kissed him quickly. "Yeah, we're having a conversation after this."

6

*C*row waited with his crew, Finn, and the medics while the Charybdis Station soldiers slipped into the Malone estate. His eyes kept slipping back to Finn. *My mate is hiding something.*

Crow hadn't meant to get so chatty on the shuttle, but Finn was surprisingly easy to talk to. Now that he'd shared some about himself, he wanted to know everything about Finn. What was his past like? Did he have a big family? What were his friends like? Now wasn't the time to ask those questions. Unfortunately.

"Exactly what traps are they laying?" Parker asked quietly.

"We timed the patrols from last night, so we're laying stun traps at the places the patrols were at particular times. If everything goes right, we can take out the patrols outside of the estate in one swoop. Then inside, we're sabotaging their shields and vehicles and the pulse cannons they have mounted to the towers. We're also gassing the barracks. We won't catch everyone, of course, but we'll take out a good number of their forces before we attack."

Parker nodded, face impressed. "Damn, boss. Your mate is kind of scary."

Crow smiled widely. "I like it."

Finn flushed, then curled into his side. "I didn't plan this all alone. I have some good captains."

Hmm, my fluffball doesn't realize how good he is. Crow leaned over and nuzzled behind Finn's furry ear, enjoying a moment of quiet while they waited.

Exactly one hour later, all of the soldiers were back, and Finn had his tablet ready. "First the patrols."

Crow saw flashes of light in the darkness but didn't hear anything.

"Now, the barracks."

Panicked voices carried from the walls of the estate and shields were immediately activated around and over the main buildings of the estate.

"Now, the pulse cannons."

Crow watched through the scope of his rifle as each of the pulse cannons overloaded from the electrical charges.

Finn tapped a few more buttons. "The rest of the charges for the shields and vehicles."

Small explosions came from the large shuttle port near the entrance, and the shields deactivated around the buildings.

"Let's go folks." Finn raised his hand. "Stay in contact and keep yourself alive."

Crow stayed beside his mate while the Charybdis

soldiers activated their shields and slipped away in the dark.

Crow waved to Parker, and together they raised their rifles and started taking out the security on the walls. He was vaguely aware of the rest of his team following suit.

Eventually, security started firing back, so they activated their shields and headed into the estate. Crow kept a hand buried in the back of Finn's shirt so he wouldn't lose him.

His mate was pretty good with his phasers. He quickly picked off any of the enemy soldiers that approached, firing shot after shot into their shields to deactivate them before finishing the soldiers off.

"Impressive, Finn," he whispered.

"That was Rufus," Finn whispered back, sounding amused. "I told you he's good backup."

Crow snorted and focused on the fighting. He chose targets far off and took as many as he could out. Unfortunately, the fighting reached a peak at the entrances of the main house and the Charybdis Station soldiers had to activate visibility to prevent being hit by friendly fire.

Finn's shield shimmered, then Crow could see him completely. His mate leaned up and kissed him. "Be careful." Finn turned to the fighting and crouched low.

"What are you doing?" Crow asked, firing his rifle towards his target near the window of the estate.

Finn didn't answer. Instead, he leapt high into the air and landed on the back of a soldier trying to slice through Brisco. He slit the man's throat and practically somersaulted through the air to cut down another of the estate soldiers.

Rufus trailed after him, firing into the bodies below the bot.

"What the fuck?" Parker's words echoed Crow's thoughts. Neither of them had time to figure out how Finn had done it.

Crow found a good perch and focused on taking out as many of the soldiers as he could. He was shit with a blade but was a damn good shot. He focused on a man inching toward Finn and fired into his shield until it was down, then took the headshot.

Crow's neck and shoulders ached from tension by the time the fighting was over. Finn was good, really good, but Crow's heart pounded each and every time someone attacked his mate.

He tapped his comm. "Headcount."

Each of his team members checked in. There were injuries, but no deaths. *Thank the gods.*

Parker scrambled onto the roof and crouched next to him. "Finn's good, boss. He moves like he's dancing."

Crow grunted. *Good fighters die all the time.*

"The fighting is over. Don't you want to go check on him?"

Crow mumbled under his breath.

"Huh?"

"I said I can see him from here. He's okay." Finn was currently directing his soldiers in securing the estate survivors and the medics in helping the injured. Crow's mate rubbed a small coin between his fingers, face pensive.

Parker sighed and bumped him with his shoulder. "Boss, what's the problem?"

"He didn't need me." The words were out of his mouth before he could stop them.

His friend's laughter didn't make Crow feel any better.

Crow shoved Parker. "Shut up."

Parker's eyes twinkled as he chuckled. "Finn isn't just cute, is he?"

Crow couldn't stop his smile. "No."

"Then what's the problem?" Parker watched him curiously.

"You see that soldier down there?" Crow pointed toward a tall and muscular Dedril in a Charybdis Station uniform. The man's eyes followed Finn even as he cuffed and secured another of Malone's soldiers.

Parker scowled. "He's eye fucking your mate." He raised his rifle. "I'll shoot him."

Crow laughed and pushed Parker's rifle back down. "No killing the good guys."

"I was just going to shoot him in the leg," Parker grumbled. "He'd live."

"He's better with a blade than me. He watched Finn's back while I stayed up here." Crow sat back and moved his rifle to his lap. "Finn didn't need me. He had that guy."

Parker groaned and flopped onto his back. "You're really going out of your way to convince yourself Finn would be better off without you."

"What the hell does that mean?"

"You've never been wrapped up in being a macho

man before." Parker glared at him. "Now you're doubting yourself because your mate didn't need you to rescue him?"

Crow made a face. "I'm doing that, aren't I?"

"Yes." Parker kicked him. "You're afraid of your feelings, so you're preparing to push him away. Don't be a dick, boss. The way you look at him is special. Give it a try."

Crow looked back down. Finn's brow was furrowed, and he wore a scowl. "Maybe he does need me."

"Maybe it doesn't matter if he *needs* you or not." Parker kicked him again. "He *wants* you. Stop acting like my teenage brother and go to him, dipshit."

Crow kicked his friend back, then crawled down the wall of the building. *I'm not a fucking teenager. I just had some legitimate concerns. We talked it out like adults because that's what I am. An adult.*

A shot fired into the ground right next to the Dedril and the man startled.

"Whoops, sorry about that!" Parker waved from the roof, looking convincingly apologetic. "Rifle misfired."

Crow grinned. *Maturity is overrated.*

Finn saw him, and his face immediately brightened. "There you are. That was some nice shooting."

Crow flushed. "Thanks. You're good with a blade."

Finn patted the hilt of his vibroblade. "You should see Selene and Draif go at it. It's fun." He snuggled against his side. "A team already secured the house from the back. Verulo is cuffed but I'm not sure what to do with him. We don't typically take prisoners."

"We can ask Jada." Crow tightened his arm around Finn when the Dedril passed them. "Free his slaves and confiscate his estate and other belongings on Rueal. He doesn't have any kids, but there are some cousins, I think. Maybe hand everything except the slaves over to them?"

Finn nodded, looking thoughtful. "Okay. I'll talk to Jada about it. We're about to go find the slaves. Do you want to come?"

Crow nodded and walked with him through the wreaked estate. "Have the other groups checked in yet?"

Finn nodded, looking pleased. "Most surrendered immediately, but those that didn't have been taken out. We took the longest."

Donna, Bertie, and the others were all huddled together in the slave quarters. Crow could almost feel the shiver of fear that filled most of them.

Finn stopped in front of the group and smiled. "Donna? Bertie?"

The two slaves stood slowly.

"You really did it." Donna started to smile. "You really came."

"Are we free?" Bertie asked.

Finn nodded. "As of right now, you belong to Charybdis Station, and we do not tolerate slavery. You will each be freed and offered a place somewhere. We'll talk more once we leave. Right now, I need you all to gather any belongings you have. Also, is our missing Vextonian here?"

Donna stooped down and helped a small, battered

woman stand. The Wello hybrid's face was bruised, and her eyes were swollen from crying.

Finn gasped. "Berenna?"

The woman stared at him suspiciously. "Who are you?"

Crow stayed close to Finn when he moved through the slaves to stand in front of the woman. His mate looked like he was about to cry.

"I've been tasked with finding you and the others that were stolen away. I haven't found Ezvin yet, but I will." Finn hesitated for a moment, then took her hand in his. "Ival will be so happy to hear you're alive. He searched for you and Ezvin after you were taken but couldn't find you."

Berenna eyes filled, and she fell into Finn's arms. "Can I see him? Oh gods, he'll never forgive me. They took Ezvin from me."

Crow wanted to hit something, but all he could do was stand there. *I can't look away from this shit, can I, Dad?*

"Come on, Berry girl. I'll help you pack." Donna wrapped an arm around the woman's shoulders. "You can tell me all about Ival and Ezvin while we do. That son of a bitch can't get mad about us talking now, can he?"

Berenna shook her head. "No, he can't."

Finn swallowed hard and watched them go. He leaned into Crow and looked up at him, eyes full of tears. "Ival sends me messages almost daily, Crow. I can finally tell him I found her."

"Maybe Ezvin is with one of the other groups on

Rueal." Crow had a bad feeling. It wasn't normal to separate slave children from their parents. It was much more profitable to pay a little more for the children and either use or sell them at a later date.

A few hours later, the last group of former slaves left on a transport for the spaceport and Finn's ship.

Finn was practically vibrating with energy. "We have so much to do. We need to process everyone and start crosschecking our lists to see who we've found. The Lord Admiral will be happy we didn't lose anyone and found so many. Then there are the newly freed slaves. I need to get them somewhere safe."

Crow shuffled his feet. "I, uh, guess I'll see you tomorrow?"

Finn narrowed his eyes. "Where do you think you're going?"

Crow fought back a smile. "Home?"

Finn didn't seem too pleased with that idea. "My quarters are really comfortable and it's late. You probably shouldn't drive a shuttle after all that fighting."

Crow tapped his chin. "Hmm, you may be right. Would you mind if I stayed with you tonight?"

Finn smiled widely. "It's the responsible thing to do."

7

A few hours later, Finn struggled to keep his eyes open. It had been a long day, and all he wanted to do was go back to his quarters and see what his mate was doing. *Maybe I shouldn't have left him alone to snoop.*

"I can't believe we did it." Wyther's smile was almost predatory. "We found all six-hundred and fifty-eight Vextonians on Rueal and freed a quarter million more."

Moyra whooped. "Now, this is a good start, everyone."

"Leti is going to be busy for a while." Finn smiled. While some of the newly freed slaves had requested a shuttle to Tammol or Aruta, a good portion wanted to go to Charybdis Station.

Nora, the lead medical doctor in the med bay, paused as she walked past him. "Lieutenant, you look like you're about to fall asleep on your feet. Our visitors have been sorted and are getting the help they need. Why don't you go get some rest?"

"That's a good idea, Nora," Weber said, eyeing Finn. "From what I hear, you were in the thick of the fighting."

Nora arched a brow. "As were you, Captain. Perhaps you, Captain Wyther, and Captain Moyra should get some rest too."

Finn grinned when the other three groaned. "We all will, Nora. Thank you." He waited until she was gone before turning back to the others. "This is the first step, but we have a lot more to do. Nora's right though. We all need rest. I'll have Ignali notify all the captains to meet with me first thing in the morning to plan our next step. Get to bed."

Moyra arched a brow. "Not all of us have a handsome man waiting on us. Maybe we want to wind down first."

Finn tried not to preen. "He is handsome, isn't he?"

Weber rolled his eyes. "On that note, good night."

Finn waved them away as he practically bolted to his room. Even though he was exhausted, he was also eager to spend some time with his mate. They had so much to learn about one another, and he wanted another kiss, damn it.

Crow relaxed in a chair, freshly showered and dressed in one of Finn's larger silk robes. He was on Finn's personal tablet.

"Hey, how did you get into my tablet? I left it locked." Finn narrowed his eyes. "Are you snooping?"

Crow looked up and smirked. "Yes, I am. I called Gus, and he helped me unlock it."

Finn huffed. "Why would he do that?"

Crow shrugged. "You're my mate, and I need to know as much about you as I can. Plus, he said something about you telling a woman named Doris that he wanted to have her babies."

Finn flushed. "I may have had too much to drink, but to be fair, he *does* want to have her babies."

Crow shook his head but kept his eyes on Finn's tablet. "You have a lot of pictures here from Charybdis Station. They go back for years. I don't see any from Cardinal's Hold."

Finn groaned. "We're back to that, huh?"

Crow looked up, smiling. "Yeah. Then we'll discuss all the delicious lingerie you have."

Heat filled Finn's face. "You really did snoop, didn't you?"

"Yep." Crow nodded toward the aerial silks. "Those are particularly interesting."

Finn could already see himself performing for Crow, and his dick started perking up. "We could go straight to those."

Crow shook his head. "Take a little time to shower and relax. Then we're talking."

Finn made a face and stomped toward the bathroom. "I'm only showering because I want to, not because you told me to."

Crow smiled. "Noted."

Finn took his time in the shower, enjoying the heated water on his sore muscles. He'd never admit it to her, but Moyra's training sessions had come in handy today. He'd gotten a little lax in his own training while Hack and Selene had been gone.

By the time he finished his shower and was dressed in his favorite pair of dark blue lace boy shorts, exhaustion was pushing him, and he fought to keep his eyes open.

"Wow." Crow's eyes widened when Finn left the bathroom. "I'm a lucky man, Finn."

Finn smiled and spun in a circle. "Like what you see?"

"Very much." Crow set the tablet down and patted his leg. "Come here, fluffball. Tell me about your family. I didn't see any pictures of you as a kid here."

Finn hissed, ears flattening. "Do we really have to do this?"

Crow's dark eyes looked sad for a moment. "I told you about my dad, Finn. My mom doesn't much like me right now, and my brother just wants to forget everything that happened on Rueal. Tell me about your family. Please?"

Finn's shoulders slumped, but he gave in and climbed onto his mate's lap. Crow was the most comfortable seat in the entire galaxy, and Finn really hoped he got to keep him.

"I don't have a family. Never did." Finn rubbed his face on Crow's shoulder. "I lived with a lot of families but ran away when I was ten. I hated feeling like a burden to people, and that's all I was to those people."

Crow's arms tightened around him. "Damn. I'm sorry, Finn. My family has its problems, but I had a good childhood."

Finn nipped the underside of Crow's chin. "I met

Amelia when I was ten. She owned a brothel near one of the spaceports."

Crow stiffened. "Please tell me she didn't –"

"She didn't sell me," Finn interrupted him. "She took me in and gave me a job in the kitchens. When I got older and wanted to work with the clients, she refused to let me. Instead, she trained me on the silks and let me perform."

Crow looked again at the silks, his expression sober. "How old were you?"

"She started training me when I was thirteen, but I didn't perform until I was sixteen."

"That's too damn young."

"Probably," Finn agreed. "I kept pushing her to let me work. I wanted to be just like her and the kittens."

"The kittens?"

"The people that worked for Amelia." Finn settled his head on Crow's shoulder. It may be his favorite place, now that he thought about it. "She wouldn't let me get into sex work."

Crow looked conflicted. "I know why I wouldn't want you to sell yourself, but why didn't she?"

Finn chewed on his lip. "I didn't know then, and it took me a while to figure it out. I was Amelia's kid."

Crow's eyes widened. "Biological?"

Finn snorted. "No. I don't know who my bio parents are or were. Amelia basically adopted me. The thing is, she didn't know anything about raising a kid, and I didn't know anything about family. She wanted better for me because she loved me."

"What happened?"

"When I was seventeen, a Charybdis Station recruiter came around. Amelia invited him in and made me talk to him. Before I knew it, I was leaving Cardinal's Hold." Finn's eyes watered. "I missed Amelia and the kittens a lot more than I realized I would. Everything was so different on Charybdis Station."

Crow stroked a hand down his back. "There's a lot of pictures of happy people on your tablet."

Finn smiled. "I met Dannol in basic training. He's my best friend. Kind of like Parker is yours."

Crow leaned back. "Whoa now. Parker isn't my best friend. He's my sidekick."

Finn snorted. "I'm so telling him you said that."

Crow chuckled. "Okay, so he might be my best friend."

"Soon after I arrived, Dannol and I met Selene. She was a legend on Charybdis Station even then. We would sneak into her practice sessions and watch her. She knew we were there, of course. After a few sessions, she made us start training with her. When we were finished with basic training, Hack took us on as crew. The Blue Solace became my family."

"What happened to Amelia and her kittens?"

Finn grabbed his tablet and scrolled through his pictures. "See this Cardinal here?"

The picture was of a middle-aged Cardinal woman with bright orange hair and ears. She stood behind a bar in what Crow had heard was one of the best clubs on Charybdis Station.

Crow's eyes brightened, and he grinned. "Please tell me that's her."

"Yep." Finn smiled softly. "She sold the brothel to one of her top kittens and retired to Charybdis Station. She tends bar at the best club in the galaxy."

"Does she know she's your mom?"

Finn laughed. "It took a while, but we figured our relationship out. We don't spend buckets of time together or anything, but she's mine and I'm hers."

Crow kissed his forehead. "I'm glad you have someone."

Finn leaned back and narrowed his eyes. "I have more than one someone, Aiden. You're mine now too."

Crow was quiet for a moment, brow furrowed in thought. "How can we, Finn? You have a life on Charybdis Station, and everything I am is on Rueal."

Finn studied him carefully. Crow's eyes were tired and tension pulled at his mouth. Finn's mate looked ready to run. He smoothed his hands over Crow's cheeks and pulled his face down for a kiss, letting his tongue dart between Crow's lips. When that kiss ended, he took another, then another.

Soon, neither of them was thinking of anything other than the taste of one another and the feel of their bodies pressed together.

Finn straddled Crow's lap and slid his hands over Crow's shoulders, pushing his mate's robe off. He hummed happily when he saw Crow was naked underneath.

His mate had plenty of muscles and thick, meaty thighs. Crow's dick was hard and more than a handful.

Finn wrapped his fingers around Crow's length and pumped, enjoying the silken heat in his hands. Crow groaned and cupped Finn's face, kissing him again. *I think I could live on his kisses.*

Finn lost track of time, his mind and body focused on Crow. He stroked his dick a few more times, then cupped Crow's balls in one hand, testing the weight against his palm.

As their kisses grew more heated, Finn's hand slipped farther down, and he ran a finger over Crow's hole, then rubbed it for a moment before dipping the tip of one finger inside him.

Crow pulled back from their kiss, panting. "You in me or me in you?"

Finn blinked, surprised. "I get a choice?" Most of the men he had been with were bigger than him, and they all automatically assumed he'd be the bottom. Usually, he had to work them up to letting him top.

Crow's laugh was rough. "Finn, I'm fucking gone on you. As long as I'm with you, as long as our bodies are moving together, I'm happy."

Finn kissed him again, deep and hard. "You drive me crazy, Aiden."

He slipped off Crow's lap and pulled him to his feet before leading him to the bed. Finn dug around for the lube before joining his mate.

Finn stretched out alongside him. He ran his hands over Crow's chest and across his stomach, noting the pale birthing line on his muscled stomach. He thought for a moment of a little, overly serious Aiden running around his home on Charybdis Station. *I'd have to make sure he knows how to smile.*

Crow spread his legs and pumped his dick, drawing

Finn's attention. He moved down and took his dick in his mouth, moaning at the taste of Crow's precum.

Crow cupped his head and pumped into Finn's mouth. "I'm close, Finn."

Finn hummed, wrapping his tongue around the tip of his shaft and sucking. He slid Crow's dick as far down his throat as he could. When he felt Crow beginning to shudder, he relaxed his throat and drank every drop as his mate came.

Crow collapsed back against the blankets, and Finn grabbed the lube. He took his time stretching Crow's hole, teasing him with his fingers and tongue. By the time Finn pushed inside him, Crow was hard again.

Finn pumped his hips, moving slowly in and out of Crow's ass. His hands clutched Crow's plump, generous ass cheeks. *My mate is pure perfection.*

He stroked Crow's dick as he moved inside him, angling his hips to hit Crow's prostate as often as he could. Crow's eyes rolled back in his head, and Finn knew he'd found the right spot. A few strokes later, Crow came hard, splattering cum all over Finn's hand.

Finn grinned and let himself go, coming hard and filling Crow's ass. As soon as his mate's ass had milked his dick of every last drop he had to give, Finn collapsed on top of him, panting hard.

Crow stroked his wet back, and Finn pressed his head against Crow's chest, listening to his fast heart beats. "Damn, Finn."

"We fit together, don't we?"

Crow was silent for several minutes, and Finn

started to worry that his mate wasn't feeling the powerful emotions moving between them.

"We fit," Crow said. "I've never felt so attached to someone, and it's just been a couple of days. I'm not... This isn't me, Finn. I'm not this man you think I am."

Finn looked at him, his heart starting to slow from its own furious pace. "What are you talking about?"

"I don't help people." Crow turned his face away. "I don't make things better. I worry about my profit line. That's who I am."

Finn struggled not to laugh. "Really? Is that why you helped Draif against Humans First? Is that why you helped lead the fight here on Rueal to get them off the planet? For your profit line? Has all that helped your smuggling business?"

Crow's confused and lost look sobered Finn quickly. "I don't know, Finn. I was so mad at them. Dad was a good person. He made the world a better place just by existing, but he's dead and I'm alive. It's not fair."

Crow's eyes filled with tears, and Finn wrapped his arms around his mate, holding him as he sobbed.

"Shh, I know it's not fair." Finn's own eyes watered, and he wished he had his medallion.

They rocked for several moments before Crow's tears slowed. "Fuck, this is embarrassing. I have the best sex of my life, then I cry all over my mate."

Finn's laugh sounded wet. "It's been a wild couple of days, handsome." He rubbed his cheek against Crow's. "I want to show you something."

He scrambled out of the bed and ran to the

bathroom. His medallion sat on the counter. He took it back to Crow and jumped into the bed, bouncing Crow around.

"Fuck, I found the wet spot," Crow grumbled before moving over. "My ass itches."

Finn patted his chest. "It's moments like this that love is built on."

Crow gave him a half smile, eyes still sad. "What did you want to show me?"

Finn held up the medallion. "I met a woman a few years ago named Hazel. It was right at the start of everything that happened with the Crellic Queen and Humans First. We rescued her from a Concord ship where she was being abused. I carried her onto our ship myself. She was so scared."

Crow scowled. "They were a nasty bunch. Their admiral had connections here on Rueal."

"Yeah." Finn swallowed hard. "Hazel joined the Blue Fleet. She wanted to help people like we had helped her. We became good friends. We hung out all the time, and I even introduced her to Amelia. Last year, she met this man and wanted to impress him, so she made me train her on the silks. We had to work around both our schedules, but she was getting good and starting to feel more confident in herself. I gave her this charm and told her she had graduated Finn's Silk Training course."

Crow wiped tears from Finn's face, and he realized he was crying. "What happened, Finn?"

"Hazel's ship left to go fight the Crellic Queen. She didn't come back." Finn shook his head, angry at his tears. "It wasn't fair either, Aiden. She was just discovering herself and truly learning to live and be happy. Now, she's just ashes on the planet she died on. Some creature pulled her apart as she screamed. She deserved better. She deserved to find her mate and dance for him. She deserved a future."

This time Crow held him as he cried. Finn sobbed against his shoulder, unable to stop the pain. He hadn't talked to anyone about Hazel. At the time, Dannol was three systems away and worried sick about Meggie. Everyone else had other things to worry about, and Finn had pushed it all away.

Then the fleet that had left to deal with the Queen came home. Morgan had given him Hazel's charm and something had broken inside him. He had lost friends before. It was part of the life of a mercenary, but none had hit him so hard.

Finn's sobs lessoned, and they clung to each other in silence for a long time. Finn knew nothing had changed for them. Crow's dad and Hazel were still dead, and Finn and Crow were still bound to two different places.

Somehow, though, it felt better to cry and mourn with someone. Life wasn't fair and that wouldn't change, but it was easier to bear when Crow was at his side.

8

*C*row woke up the next morning with a smile on his face. It had been a long time since he had felt at peace. Maybe not since he was a kid who soaked up his dad's stories and ideas but had no idea what the galaxy was really like.

The bed was empty, but a tray of food sat on the table next to a wall of glass looking over the dock. Finn's medallion and communicator weren't on the bedtable anymore either. *My mate has a lot to do.* Crow still wished he had said goodbye.

His comm chimed, and he leaned over to grab it, careful to keep the video off. "Crow here."

"Hey, boss. You still at Finn's place?" Parker's voice held more than a little amusement.

Crow cleared his throat, cheeks heating. "I'm on the Blue Albatross, yes."

"*Where* on the Blue Albatross?" Parker teased.

Crow grinned and rubbed the sleep from his eyes. "What did you need, Parker?"

"One of our contacts has some goods he wants to sell us outright. He already brought them over. It's all sitting in storage."

"That's strange." Crow frowned. Typically, merchants contracted him to smuggle goods off to sell for them. They avoided paying tariffs and could make a higher profit.

"Yeah. He's closing his business in Rueal. Said he'd come back when Jada had shit straightened out."

Crow sighed. "Leaving doesn't help anything."

"You know business has been off since HF deported so many. When you add in the fighting, it's hard to make a living right now." Parker sounded tired. "That will change, but it takes time. Some folks don't want to wait."

"I'll come home now and look over what they have for us." Crow rolled out of bed and started pulling on his clothes. *So much for some down time with Finn.* "Do me a favor and ask Brisco to start gathering info on the Weasel. He has a large group of Vextonians, and Finn will need as much information as possible. We need to locate his base if possible."

"Hmm." Parker sounded amused again. "I thought we were going to hand over info to Charybdis Station and then get back to work? It sounds like we're getting involved here."

Crow rolled his neck and shoulders, trying to work the kinks out. "We're involved. *Really* involved."

Parker laughed. "I hear you, boss. I'll see you when you get home."

Crow pulled his boots on and grabbed his rifle,

slinging it over his back. His eyes lingered on the aerial silks and his dick hardened. *I'd give every credit I have to see Finn on those.*

He shook his head and left the room.

Finn sat in one of his office chairs, legs folded beneath him. A tired-looking Fallon woman sat in the chair next to him. Her long, golden hair was gathered in a messy bun on top of her head, and her Charybdis Station uniform was wrinkled. Screens were pulled up around the two.

Finn smiled when he saw him, his golden eyes lighting up with pleasure. "Aiden, did you sleep well?"

Crow moved closer and leaned down to give Finn a kiss. His body told him he needed to stay right there and kiss Finn all day.

He forced himself to pull back. "What's the plan for today? I have a few things to take care of this morning, but if you need help this afternoon, I'm in."

Finn pulled him down for another kiss. When the woman next to him cleared her throat, Finn pulled back. "Aiden, this is Halli."

The Fallon sent him a wry look. "Hello, Mr. Crow. Everyone in the blue fleet has heard about you and Finn. It's a pleasure to meet you."

Crow flushed. "Nice to meet you, ma'am."

Finn chuckled and gently nipped Crow's lip before settling back in his seat, looking far too satisfied. "We're updating our numbers and putting together our reports today. I've already sent requests for information on Dramacus, Prism, and the Weasel. I don't want to make a move until we know more."

Crow knew Prism was the only moon circling Rueal that was settled. It was an industrial colony and produced a lot of the luxury items Rueal exported. Dramacus was a planet in the Sugarworm system but was a bit of a mystery. The Weasel though...

"Brisco is gathering intel on the Weasel too. I'll let you know what he finds." Crow cupped Finn's face. "I'll call you later today. Be careful."

"You too."

Crow left the office reluctantly. Even as a hormone-driven teenager, he had never been so drawn to someone before. He wanted to stay right at Finn's side. For the first time in his life, he was reluctant to go home. Normally, when he was confused or worried, he'd talk to his dad. *Damn it.*

He left the spaceport and found his speeder parked near the entrance where Brisco had left it. As soon as he put his helmet on and pulled out, he lifted into the air. Speeders weren't ideal for flying, but Parker had taken the rest of Crow's team home in the shuttle last night.

He flew over Pagent's Distillery, absently noting that someone was already repairing the city defenses. Jada had temporarily commandeered an abandoned business building to serve as the government center. For some reason, his friend thought she ought to update Crow every time she did anything so his comm stayed full of messages.

He thought for a minute, then made a call.

"Hey, man." Dermot's voice filled his helmet. "I

called last night, and Staci said you and the others were out rescuing slaves."

Crow licked his lips. "Yeah. Some missing Vextonian slaves."

"The ones Charybdis Station ordered released?" Dermot sounded impressed.

"Yeah, those. Dermot, I need to ask you something and please be honest."

"Sure." His brother sounded surprised. Dermot was the oldest, but Crow seldom asked him for anything.

"When you met Jenise, you knew she was your mate immediately, right?"

"Yeah. I felt a humming, just like a Havenite. Dad said he felt the same when he met Mom." Crow could hear the smile in Dermot's voice. "We may be galaxy mutts, but genetics are a funny thing. Mom has Havenite blood too, but she didn't sense anything. She always said she had too much damn human blood."

"I didn't hear a hum, but there was this loud beating. Like I could hear the pulse of his heart." Crow swallowed hard. "It filled my head, and it's like my heart started beating to match his."

"Aiden! You met your mate?" Excitement practically vibrated through the audio in his helmet. "That sounds a bit like the hum I heard. Damn, little brother. I'm so happy for you. You need some good in your life."

Crow couldn't hold back his grin. "His name is Finn, and he's with Charybdis Station. He's searching for a large number of the Vextonians that were given to Teresa Malone, then went missing."

"That's some nasty business. Lucky you're good at that shit."

Crow blinked, surprised. *Good at rescuing people? Not my thing.* "What do you mean?"

"You know, all that dangerous shit. You're good at helping people out of bad situations." Dermot paused for a minute. "Dad told me about all the slaves you and he smuggled off planet. Don't pretend you're not one of the good guys, Aiden."

Crow's laugh was hollow, even to his own ears. "I'm not one of the good guys, Dermot."

Dermot groaned. "How are we arguing about this? You help people all the time, Aiden. You smuggle slaves to freedom off planet, yeah, but you also go out of your way to take care of your family and friends. Sure, you dodge tariffs and make a profit, but you don't cheat people. You're a good person, just accept it and move on."

Crow didn't know what to say. He didn't see what his brother did, but he was tired of arguing with people about it. If Finn, Parker, and Dermot wanted to think he was a good guy, Crow wasn't going to go out of his way to prove them wrong.

"You still there?" Dermot asked. "Don't let Mom get in your head, Aiden. She's not herself right now."

Crow snorted. "That's the truth. You seen the house?"

"Yeah. Jenise and I went over last night and cleaned it. I took care of the lawn too. You remember when she grounded us for a week when we left the dishes unwashed for the weekend?"

Crow laughed. "She was always so proud of the house."

"I think it's hard for her to be there." Dermot sighed. "Jenise and I are thinking of moving in with her. Your friend Jada is already trying to put Pagent's Distillery back together, and we'll be voting in a new president of Rueal soon. I think I'll try to rebuild Dad's company."

"I thought you didn't want anything to do with it?" Crow asked, surprised.

"I wanted to make my own company, not inherit one." Dermot sounded sad. "Now, I think I'd like to see Dad's company back in business and stronger than ever. It would still be mine, but I like that it would be his too. Does that make sense?"

"It does." Crow smiled softly. He liked the idea of Dermot and Jenise building a family in the old house and making Dad's company his again. "Let me know if I can be of any help."

"I will. Just make sure you visit Mom as much as possible. Jenise and I can't seem to break through her walls. Maybe you can."

"I doubt it, but I'll keep trying."

"I want to meet your mate too. Can you bring him to dinner tonight at Mom's? Jenise will cook something nice."

"I'll see if he can and let you know."

"Good." Dermot sounded pleased. "Be careful out there, little brother."

Crow thought about Dermot's words for the rest of the drive home. He had always tried to keep his life simple – take care of business and stay under the radar. When his dad died, everything had changed. Now, he wasn't sure which direction to go. *Keep it simple and go back to how things were before or complicate the shit out of everything and keep Finn?*

"Keep Finn," he muttered. "Fucking keep Finn."

He made another call.

"Do you miss me already?" Finn asked, voice full of mischief. "I miss you."

Crow grinned. "Dinner with my family tonight?"

"Was that an invitation?"

"Yeah."

"Send me the address." Finn sounded nervous. "Will they be mad if I intrude?"

"You are not an intrusion, Finn. My brother wants to meet you."

"Okay." Finn sounded shy. "I'll be there."

By the time he was home, his mind was settled. He would figure out how to be the mate Finn deserved.

Parker met him in front of the largest storage building. "Hey, boss. Wait until you see what Tomin has for us."

Crow grunted and followed his friend inside. He was happy to see his crew was already inventorying everything and packing it tightly.

"He has two hundred crates of fabric that will sell for a bundle." Parker practically rubbed his hands together. "Then he has sixty-two crates of Pagent's whiskey, which you know will bring in some credits. The rest are high-end luxury items."

"I think we can move this." Crow nodded in approval. "Finish the inventory, then offer a fair price."

A loud yowl drew Crow's attention, and he moved farther into the building. "What was that?"

Parker rolled his eyes. "That was a luxury item I wish Tomin hadn't offered us."

A few rows down, a large crate shook as another loud yowl and hissing assaulted their ears. Joelle was trying to look inside, but a large black paw reached through the bars of the door to swat at her.

Crow crouched down in front of the door and was met with a pair of glowing blue eyes. "A glimmer?"

The species from Grellweir had a longer, more scientific, name, but the large winged felines were more commonly called glimmers. The beast was crammed into the crate, but Crow thought it was more cub than adult. Its thick black and blue fur was fluffed up in irritation, and its wings were folded up close to its sides.

"It's not happy." Joelle tried to approach again, but the glimmer hissed.

"Glimmers sell well as companion pets." Parker grimaced. "This one acts like it would rather maul someone than cuddle."

Crow smiled. "I should send it to Draif's friend Leti."

The glimmer growled, and the crate shook again. Parker gave him a look. "Yes, I'm sure his mate, the infamous Will Hackett, would appreciate that."

Joelle started laughing. "You ought to gift it to your mate, boss. At least he wouldn't set you on fire."

Crow laughed too, but the more he thought of it, the more he liked the idea. He could see Finn and him curled up on one of the decadent sofas in his quarters, the glimmer happily sleeping on the floor beside them.

"Once you've fed, watered, and walked it, Joelle, load it in the shuttle. I'll let Finn look at it tonight. He might want to keep it."

She glared at him. "Okay, boss. I'll just risk life and limb and do that right now."

He grinned widely. "Thanks."

As he walked away, he heard her mutter. "I hope Finn *does* set you on fire."

———

CROW STOOD WITH DERMOT AND HIS MOM AND WATCHED the crate shake in the back of the shuttle. He had arrived thirty minutes ago, but the beast hadn't calmed down yet.

Jenise was finishing dinner while Dermot and he tried to figure out how to get the glimmer into the house to surprise Finn.

"That is the worst mating gift I've ever seen." His mom scowled when the glimmer hissed. "Aiden, do you secretly want to kill your mate?"

Crow gave her a sheepish look. "Maybe this wasn't a good idea."

Dermot nodded furiously. "You got that right."

Crow and his brother looked a lot alike. They got their dark skin and black hair from their mom, but they both had their dad's eyes. Crow was bigger than

Dermot, but somehow his brother always made him feel more centered. *Has to be a big brother skill.*

Diana huffed, annoyed. "I'm going back inside. You can deal with this mess." Her house shoes slapped against the walk. She was dressed in the same clothes she'd been wearing the last time he'd visited, and she clearly hadn't showered in a while.

Crow waited until she was inside. "I'm worried about Mom."

Dermot sighed. "Me too. We're trying, but Mom has to want to try too, and she just doesn't."

"You remember when you brought Jenise home that first time?"

Dermot grinned. "Mom made dinner and fussed over her all night." His smile faded. "I'm sorry, Aiden. Jenise is cooking a good meal, and we cleaned the house up."

Crow shrugged. "You said it before. Mom isn't herself right now."

A shuttle landed in the open space beside them, and Dermot gave him a panicked look. "We haven't gotten the hiss beast into the house yet!"

Finn opened the shuttle door and bounced out, grinning widely. He wore an elegant black sleeveless shirt with a golden chain belt. Tight black pants were tucked into shiny boots. Gold armbands encircled his muscular biceps, and a gold cuff earring decorated one of his fuzzy ears. His bushy tail whipped back and forth behind him, and his eyes shone brightly in the near dark evening.

He smiled shyly at Dermot. "You must be Aiden's brother."

Dermot's mouth was still hanging open as he stared at Finn.

Crow growled and not so gently tapped his brother's chin, closing his mouth. "This is Dermot. He's mated and not nearly as good in bed as I am."

Dermot gave him a disgruntled look. "I'm great in bed. Just ask Jenise."

Finn laughed. "Oh gods, you two are definitely brothers." His eyes fell on the crate. "What's that?"

"Nothing." Crow moved to stand in front of the crate, then jumped when the glimmer swatted him. "Damn it!"

Finn's eyes widened, and he gasped. "Is that a Grellweir glimmer? It's beautiful." He reached out and unlatched the crate. "You poor baby. Why are you locked in that tiny crate?"

Crow and Dermot both called out, but it was too late. The door opened, and the snarling monster leapt out.

9

*F*inn stood in Crow's childhood home, Roxy cuddled in his arms. He swayed slowly and cooed into the poor glimmer's ear. As soon as he had opened the cage, the large winged feline had flown into his arms, mewling pitifully.

Crow's brother watched him from the couch. "I can't believe that thing didn't claw your face off."

Crow elbowed him hard. "Don't give it ideas."

Finn narrowed his eyes on his mate. "Roxy isn't an 'it.' She's a beautiful baby glimmer."

Crow smiled widely and batted his eyes. "Yes, dear. The beast is an adorable ball of perfection."

Dermot laughed, and Finn rolled his eyes. Roxy settled her head on Finn's shoulder and purred. The glimmer would get large quickly, but right now she was a warm and heavy weight in his arms.

"Where's your mom?" Finn asked, looking around curiously. The house was nice and comfortable. It was clearly made for a family, and Finn loved the photos in the frames above the fireplace. *Little Aiden was a cutie.*

Crow and Dermot exchanged a nervous look.

Before they could answer, a young Wello-Dedril hybrid came in, a smile covering her face. "You must be Finn. I'm Jenise." She patted Dermot's shoulder. "This one's mate. Dinner is ready when you all are."

"Is Mom in there?" Dermot asked hopefully.

Jenise's smile faded. "No. She went to her room."

Finn's heart hurt for the woman. He had only known Crow for a few days, but even now, if he lost him, it would destroy Finn. "She must be tired. We can make her a plate and bring it to her."

"Yes." Dermot nodded quickly. "Good idea."

Finn settled Roxy into one of the chairs around the table, washed his hands, then sat next to her. The glimmer eyed the others with suspicion but seemed content to sit and watch them eat.

Once their plates were full and everyone was sitting, Dermot gave Finn a hard look. "Alright. Time to tell us about yourself, Finn. My baby brother is a good catch. What makes you think you're good enough for him?"

Crow looked horrified. "Dermot, what the hell?"

Finn couldn't help his smile. It made him happy that Crow's family appreciated him. "He *is* the best catch in the galaxy, and he's all mine. It's too late, Dermot. I won't give him up, so you're stuck with me, good enough or not."

Dermot smiled. "At least you know how lucky you are."

Jenise leaned forward, eyes bright. "I love your tail, Finn. It's so bushy and cute."

Finn preened. "Thank you." He nodded to Crow. "*He* hasn't complimented my tail at all."

Jenise gasped, hand pressed to her heart. "The bastard!"

Crow dropped his head to the table, groaning. "Why did I want to introduce you to my family?"

They laughed and the conversation flowed easily. Finn liked Dermot and Jenise. They were both kind, funny, and easy to talk to. He found out they were finally ready to start a family of their own, and Dermot wanted to rebuild his dad's company. Jenise was a teacher and was eager to get back to work once Pagent's Distillery was settled again.

Before he knew it, Finn was polishing off dessert. "That was so good, Jenise. I don't think I've eaten that well since I left Charybdis Station."

"Does Amelia cook dinner for you?" Jenise asked. "Diana used to cook dinner for the whole family once a week."

Finn made a face. "Amelia isn't that kind of mom. She'll cut the balls off a man if he hurts me, but she'd burn the station down if she tried to make dinner. We usually eat at Juniper's Diner."

Jenise stood and gently smacked the back of Crow's head. "You hear that? You better be nice to Finn or his mom will take care of you."

Crow gave her a sour look. "I'll guard my junk." He turned back to Finn. "Did you get a lot done today?"

Finn nodded, fighting off a yawn. "Halli and I

finished our reports and sent them off. The Green Lieutenant lent us some ships, and I sent the Vextonians on to Charybdis Station temporarily. Vextonar is in too much upheaval right now. The yellow fleet and the rest of our allies have taken out HF, but the government has completely toppled, and they didn't have a Jada to step in."

"She has made things easier here." Dermot nudged his brother. "Jada and you."

Crow looked surprised. "Me?"

Jenise put a small bowl of minced meat in front of Roxy and rolled her eyes before sitting back down. "Yeah, you. Do you think no one realizes how involved you and your crew have been?"

"We aren't helping rebuild." Crow's shoulders slumped. "We helped tear everything apart, but we haven't helped build it back up."

"Yet," Finn added. "You haven't helped *yet*. Rueal is your home, and I know you'll be there for her." It hurt him to even say the words. He loved Charybdis Station and couldn't imagine not living there, but Crow felt the same way about Rueal. *Someone will have to give up their home.*

Crow gave him a knowing look and reached across the table for his hand.

Finn swallowed hard and shoved his emotions away. "We got back some information about Dramacus and Prism." Finn had sent Moyra and her crew to scout the small moon. There were so many factories there, and they needed to narrow down where the Vextonians were.

"Good." Crow eyes were heated as they ran over Finn's face. "Anything I can help with?"

Finn flushed hot. *There are a lot of things I want your help with, handsome.* He shook his head. "Uh, I'm at a loss with Dramacus. The planet has shut down all incoming ships. They've completely isolated themselves from the rest of the galaxy, and it will be hard to get in."

"I have a contact on Dramacus." Crow squeezed his hand. "He used to live on Aruta but moved right before Dramacus shut down the spaceports. I'll get in touch with him tonight. He can help your scouts get in and find the Vextonians."

Finn felt his ears perk up. "Really? That will help." Finn could send Wyther and his crew to check it out if Crow's contact would help.

"What would Dramacus even want with Vextonian slaves?" Dermot said, shaking his head. "I can see Prism wanting them. Employment at the factories went down drastically when most of the non-humans were deported."

Finn sighed. "I have no idea. Charybdis Station never had much to do with the planet. Now, with it shutting everyone out, there's no easy way to contact them."

He watched Roxy delicately eat from the small bowl in front of her. She was such a good girl. *Too bad I'm not a good boy.*

Finn stood. "I'll be right back."

Crow tugged on his hand and frowned. "Where are you going?"

Finn rolled his eyes. "To the bathroom. Is that okay with you?"

Dermot and Jenise laughed at Crow when he hid his face. "Yeah. Sorry."

Finn patted his mate's shoulder and went into the front room, Roxy following behind him. He took a minute to use the bathroom and wash his hands. "I'm not a liar, Roxy."

His new glimmer gave him a disbelieving look and mewled softly.

"Don't judge me." He picked Roxy up and quietly slipped out of the bathroom, then tip-toed up the stairs.

There were a few bedrooms on this level, but one door was already cracked, and he could hear a vid-screen playing from within.

He poked his head in. Crow's mom sat in a chair near the window, eyes glued to the vid-screen. She looked rough, and he could smell her from the door. She looked a lot like Dermot and Crow with dark skin, a full figure, and strong features. Her Wello spots barely showed against her skin, and he knew for a fact Crow didn't have any of his own.

Finn slid into the room and shut the door.

She looked up from the screen. "You Finn?"

He nodded. "You Diana?"

"That's me." She eyed Roxy. "I see you got your gift."

"This is Roxy." He stroked a hand down Roxy's back, then settled into the chair across from Diana. "Isn't she beautiful? I've never had a pet before."

Diana shrugged and looked back at the vid-screen.

"The boys had a dog when they were younger. His name was Ralphie."

"Did they get along with him?" Finn leaned back and watched the vid-screen. It looked like the local news. They were covering the rebuilding of one of the larger cities on the other side of the planet. HF had fought hard for it, so there was a lot more to clean up than in Pagent's Distillery.

"Aiden and Dermot loved that dog. It broke their hearts when he died. Dermot moved on, but I didn't expect Aiden to ever get another pet."

"Why not?"

"His heart bruises easily." She glanced at him, then back at the vid-screen. "He tries to hide it by playing the wily bad boy, but his emotions get the better of him every time."

Finn thought about it. "I can see that. He cares about his crew a lot and goes out of his way to make sure they stay safe. It hurt him when he lost, uh, I think Parker said it was Horski and Mel."

Diana gave him a sharp look. "What do you mean?"

Finn's ears flicked in agitation, and Roxy's ears did the same. "A few days ago, he lost them. They were fighting for Pagent's Distillery."

She closed her eyes. A bitter smile hardened her features. "He didn't say anything when he came by. I didn't really give him a chance though."

"He holds a lot in." Finn stroked his tail, then Roxy's. "Sometimes it feels like his walls are too high to get past."

Diana nodded. "He hurts easily, so he's quick to

push people away. He's always been like that. It drove Perick crazy."

Finn nodded, then watched the news some more.

"I'm sorry I didn't eat dinner with you all. I didn't want to ruin things."

He shrugged. "You're hurting. It would destroy me to lose Aiden, and I just met him. You were mated for a lot longer."

"Forty-two years." She closed her eyes again and leaned her head back. "Almost every night I dream he's still alive. We talk, argue, make love, just live like we always did. Then I wake up and the bed's empty and I'm so cold. I remember he's dead and buried and I'm alone."

Finn shifted in his seat, throat thick with tears. He would sometimes dream like that about Hazel. In his dreams, they were at the club or having lunch in Juniper's Diner. She would laugh, and they'd share gossip.

Diana's sharp eyes narrowed. "You know what I mean."

"Yeah." He swallowed and wiped at his eyes. "I've lost friends. It's hard to deal with sometimes."

"I don't know what to do." She folded her hands in her lap. "I don't know how to live without him."

Finn looked around the bedroom. A man's hat sat on top of the dresser, and a pair of men's loafers were near the bed. "He's everywhere here."

She held back a sob and nodded. "I can't let him go."

Finn thought about how he couldn't go back to his favorite club without thinking of Hazel. Morgan and he had struggled to sort her things and pack up her house. "You can't stay here."

Diana looked at him like he was crazy. "What?"

Finn sniffed and wiped his eyes. "You can't let him go if you're here. This is the home you built with him."

"Where the hell would I go?"

Finn shook his head. "How should I know?"

Diana's laugh was hoarse, but amused. "You know everything else."

"Oh, if you only knew how little I really know." Finn smiled. "My life motto is 'fake it till you make it.'"

Diana snorted. "Aiden said you were a big deal from Charybdis Station."

Finn raised a brow. "I'm just the lieutenant of the blue fleet." He stopped, startled. "Oh, shit. I am a big deal."

Diana laughed, eyes brightening. "You are something else, kitty."

Finn liked the endearment. It reminded him of Amelia and the kittens.

The door opened, and Crow looked in, face confused. "Finn? I thought you were using the bathroom."

Dermot and Jenise peeked around him, equally baffled.

"I did, babe. Thanks for announcing it to the whole world." Finn winked at his mate. "Diana was just getting ready to take a shower and come down for dinner."

Diana arched a brow. "I was?"

"Yep." Finn stood and set Roxy down. "Roxy and I

are going to pack you a bag. We haven't seen Aiden's home yet. Parker said it was some fancy villa. Have you been there?"

"His smuggling headquarters?" Diana looked shocked. "Of course I haven't."

"Good, then we can look it over together and point out all the decorating mistakes he probably made." Finn eyed his mate. "Did you even decorate it or is it a stereotypical bachelor pad?"

Crow snorted. "You're criticizing me? You have aerial silks hanging in your quarters."

Dermot and Jenise's eyes grew wide.

"Do you now?" Jenise asked.

Finn flushed. "I do, but now I'm thinking I should take them down and throw them away."

Crow shook his head. "No, no, no."

Diana chuckled. "Get out of my room and let me shower and dress. I'll pack my own bag. Finn, don't forget to take that hissy monster with you."

Finn scooped Roxy up and cooed to her. "Pretty girl, they're just mean."

———

A FEW HOURS LATER, FINN AND DIANA WALKED AROUND the spacious villa. "Damn, handsome. This place is nice."

Diana nodded. "It's a bit bare, but you live here alone, so it's to be expected." She looked a lot better after showering. Finn had the feeling she hadn't left the house since her husband died. She looked overwhelmed as she gazed out the window.

"The soil isn't too good." Crow looked unsure, and Finn thought it was adorable. "A few years from now, it might be. There are several acres, and there's a lake on the southwest portion."

"Boss?" Parker came through the door. His eyes widened, and he grinned when he saw Diana. "Mrs. Crow, it's nice to see you out and about." His gaze found Finn and Roxy, and he blanched. "You brought it back? Joelle swore vengeance on the hiss beast."

Roxy purred and rubbed her head under Finn's chin. "My baby girl isn't a hiss beast. How many rooms does this place have, babe?"

The villa really was nice, if a little bare. The archways were rounded and windows were everywhere, letting in the bright sunshine. Finn opened a door near the back of the first floor and poked his head in, looking around.

Crow shrugged. "Ten bedrooms. I think. Everything's spread out."

"You think?" Diana arched a brow. "Well, you have plenty of space for kids."

Finn backed out, returning to the front room. "Kids? Shit, Aiden, I didn't think about –"

"I'm on birth control," Crow muttered, covering his face with his hands. "Fuck, this is embarrassing."

Diana snickered. "Birth control isn't a sure thing, especially with hybrids."

"Mother!"

Finn started giggling and couldn't make himself stop. Crow sounded so scandalized.

Crow glared at him, then tugged him into his arms. "Laugh now, but what will you do if I end up pregnant?"

"If it's a boy, we should name him Perick." The words were out of Finn's mouth before he could stop them.

Diana made a pained sound, eyes tearing up.

Finn rushed to her side. "I'm so sorry, Diana."

She covered her mouth and shook her head. "No. I would like that. Perick would have liked that." She wiped her eyes and grabbed his hand. "Let's explore this place, okay?"

Finn nodded, then tugged Diana over to the room he'd peeked in. "This is my office now."

"That's the library." Crow wrapped an arm around his waist.

Finn tucked himself in against Crow's side. "My office now."

They took their time exploring the house, and Finn knew when he found the right room. It was on the first floor and near the kitchen. The windows looked out over an empty backyard.

He exchanged looks with Diana, and she nodded. "This is my room now."

"Mom?" Crow looked dumbstruck. "Really?"

"I can't live alone in the house in town. Perick is everywhere there, and I can't empty my head of him." She walked into the large room. "Dermot and Jenise will make a home there, and I'll make mine here." She looked at Crow. "If you don't mind having me here, Aiden."

Crow shook his head. "No. I'm happy to have you here, Mom."

Parker whistled. "Anytime you cook, can you set another place at the table?"

Diana rolled her eyes. "You're always welcome, Parker. Tell everyone they're all welcome at my table." She looked over the empty room. "I need some things. Parker, can you take me to town?"

Parker crooked his arm and held it toward her. "Yes, ma'am."

Finn and Crow watched them leave. Finn leaned against his mate and soaked in the quiet of the house. "My house at Charybdis Station isn't this big, but it has three bedrooms. It's right next to my best friend's home."

Crow tugged him into his arms and cupped his face. "We'll figure something out, Finn. Now that I have you, I don't want to let you go."

10

*C*row cupped Finn's ass and held him still as he pushed deep inside his mate. Finn was braced on his elbows with his ass in the air while Crow took him from behind.

Crow spit hair out of his mouth when Finn's tail whacked him in the face again. He wanted to laugh, but Finn's ass felt so damn good around his dick. The groans and curses coming from Finn made him move faster.

"So close." Finn panted and pushed his hips back with each thrust. "Aiden!"

Crow let go and came hard, filling Finn's ass. Finn spasmed beneath him and gave a long, drawn-out moan as he came against the sheets.

Crow fell to the bed and rolled Finn away from the wet spot. He held Finn tightly as their breathing evened out.

"I think it gets better each time." Crow gently pulled out of Finn's ass and rolled his mate around to face him. "Can you stay tonight? I like having you in my bed."

Finn kissed his shoulder and snuggled closer. "Yeah. Ignali knows where to reach me. Right now, we're just waiting on information anyway."

Over the past week, Crow noticed Finn spent more and more time at the villa. A few of his things made their way into Crow's bedroom, including one of the long, aerial silks. Unfortunately, he hadn't managed to see Finn use it yet.

Despite the small changes, Finn's base was still the Blue Albatross, and Crow knew that couldn't be helped. His mate had a lot of Vextonians still to find.

Halli had made quite a bit of progress of her own and more were being turned over every day. Finn had also sent Wyther and his crew to Dramacus to meet with Crow's friend Duncan. They hadn't reached the planet yet, but they were close.

"Mom will probably make breakfast." Crow slowly stroked his hands up and down Finn's bare back.

"Will she have time?" Finn asked, laughing against Crow's shoulder.

Crow's mom had spent the last week immersing herself in Crow's smuggling business. It was a little embarrassing how quickly she was picking everything up. Most of his contacts officially liked her better than him.

"Maybe not. She's arranging to move some of the items we bought last week." Crow yawned.

Finn smoothed a hand over Crow's short hair. "Get some sleep, babe. I'm right here with you."

Crow gave him a drowsy smile and let himself fall asleep, content to have Finn near him.

When he woke up the next morning, Finn's side of the bed was empty. Crow scowled and rubbed sleep from his eyes before rolling out of bed.

He quickly worked through his morning routine, then dressed and headed to Finn's *office*. The library now had a large desk and several vid-screens that took up about half the room. The other half had books, a sofa, and several chairs.

Finn lay on the sofa, eyes concentrated on his tablet. Roxy stretched out atop him, and the glimmer glared at Crow as he approached. *This is not how I envisioned this going, hiss beast.*

Finn looked up, eyes brightening when he saw Crow. "Jada just left. The last city has been taken, and Rueal is officially on clean-up duty. They're going to arrange a presidential election in a few months when more of the previously deported arrive back home. The aristocratic families are throwing a fit because they've opened the elections up to *any* citizen of Rueal."

Crow grunted and fell into one of the chairs. "Why didn't you wake me? How did she get the senate to agree to that?"

Finn blew him a kiss. "I wore you out last night, and you needed the rest. She was just here for a moment. She said she'd come back this evening. As for the senate, what is left of it anyway, they're all kissing her ass in the hope she'll support one of them for president. Jada is kind of a folk hero now."

Finn's tablet buzzed, and he frowned, looking back

to it. He was silent as he read whatever was on the screen, but his body grew tense.

Crow leaned forward, bracing his arms on his knees. "What's happening?"

"Moyra found the Vextonians that were sold to the factories. They're all concentrated in *one* factory. Guess who owns it?"

Crow shrugged. "It could be any one of the aristocratic families. Several have business interests there."

"What family has been a pain in the ass for Pagent's Distillery?" Finn asked, eyes narrowed in anger.

Crow sat up quickly. "Jevio."

"Moyra has eyes on Philip Jevio as we speak." Finn slowly sat up. "His three factories and his personal estate are putting over five hundred thousand of the missing Vextonians to work. Moyra says the security is pretty lax, probably because you and Jada have taken out their resources here on Rueal. He's sitting pretty in a lavish estate while the Vextonians continue production for his businesses."

Crow's attention focused on one name. "Philip Jevio."

Finn nodded. "I'll gather my fleet and see if Leslie wants to join in. Moyra and her crew will do as much damage from within as possible."

"I want in." Crow forced himself to relax his shoulders and neck. "I'll leave my crew here and tell them to keep Mom busy, but I want in."

Finn moved to sit in his lap. "I wouldn't have it any other way. We'll go in together."

CROW WATCHED AS THEY APPROACHED PRISM, THEIR SHIP drawing closer. The moon was completely surrounded with an artificial atmosphere maintained by the aristocratic families that owned it. Within the atmosphere, hundreds of large factories and several pockets of overcrowded housing covered the surface. Here and there an estate would take up several acres, but from space, the moon looked like a dirty, industrial park.

They couldn't attack from the air because of the atmospheric shield and for the fear of harming the Vextonians below. Luckily, one of Moyra's crew, a man named Noe, had already taken one of the defensive posts and was able to let them through the shield.

"Where are we landing?" Crow asked. There were too many ships to go unnoticed for long, even if they were shielded from view.

Finn patted his knee. "We're splitting into four groups. Althea, Weber, and Ronnie will lead the attacks against the three factories. You and I are focusing on the estate. Moyra's people are spread out and ready to offer aid as they can. Each of our targets are full of innocent people, so we have to be careful."

The woman sitting in front of them turned around, and Crow grinned. "Leslie. Funny meeting you here."

The Green Lieutenant smiled widely. "Like I would let Finn have all the fun. I'm looking forward to finishing off the Jevio family. I've seen the damage they've done to Rueal."

Finn squeezed his hand and gave him a long look before turning back to Leslie. "We have too."

Finn tapped the strip of metal on his face, and Rufus appeared above them. "Moyra said the estate has the heaviest security. She's already sabotaged the shuttles and ships, so Jevio can't escape. She also made contact with some of the slaves. They're going to try to keep people out of the way once the attack begins."

Crow tried to relax in his seat as Finn addressed the soldiers and went through the expected security and their plans. Crow knew he should pay attention, but his focus was on one thing only – finding Philip Jevio and putting a hole in his head.

Leslie kept her eyes on Finn at the front of the shuttle but leaned back and tapped his knee. "What crawled up your ass, Crow? That scowl could scare away Princess Buttercup."

Crow's brow furrowed. "Princess Buttercup?"

"Not important." She waved his comment away. "What's wrong?"

Parker leaned over the seat from the back. "Boss? Is something wrong?"

"Nothing." His voice was clipped and guilt flared. "It's not important."

Brisco patted his shoulder from behind him. "I'm not convinced."

Finn finished talking, then made his way back to his seat. "I hate when they send my image to multiple ships when I'm talking. I'm always afraid one of my captains has my projection pulled up on a soldier's ass or something."

Leslie snickered. "That only happened once."

"I hate Moyra." Finn shook his head. "Leslie, I need to ask you a favor."

"Sure, whatcha need?"

"I have to lead this attack." Finn sighed. "It's my job, and I have to be there."

Leslie looked confused. "Okay?"

Finn gripped Crow's hand. "I need you to get Aiden to Jevio and watch his back. My mate deserves to be the one to put that bastard out of our misery."

Crow shook his head. "No. You're my mate, and I'll stay with you."

Finn cupped his cheek. "The man killed your dad, Aiden. You have no idea how much I want to be there for you when you face him. This is the next best thing."

He started to protest again, but Leslie leaned back and smacked his shoulder. "I'll get your man to the dickhead, Finn. Don't worry."

"We're with him too." Parker patted Finn's shoulder. "We'll keep an eye on the boss."

Finn pulled Crow's hand to his lips and placed a gentle kiss on his gloved knuckles. "Be careful and keep me updated. Aiden, I love you. I know it's fast, but I can't help it."

Leslie's eyes grew wide, and a grin spread across her face. Parker and Brisco grinned and sat back in their seats.

Crow ignored them and swallowed the lump of nerves stuck in his throat. "Damn it, Finn. Don't die, okay? I can't lose you now, and I still haven't gotten to see you do your aerial silk dance."

"Say what now?" Leslie was leaning into their space again.

"Aerial silk dance?" Brisco's head was back over the seat.

"What do you wear during this dance?" Parker asked.

Crow growled, and Brisco and Parker sat back again. Leslie ignored him.

Finn rolled his eyes and shoved the woman away. "Aiden, if you make it out of this without getting injured, I'll dance for you."

Crow gave him a smug look. "Now that's motivation to be careful."

Soon, the ship landed in a large clearing on the well-maintained estate grounds. Soldiers activated their shields, filed out of the ship, and headed toward the estate. Everyone knew their mission by this point.

Finn leaned up and kissed him. "If you die, I'll have Death bring me your soul to torture, okay?"

Crow gave him a puzzled look. "What?"

Leslie snickered and grabbed his hand. "Come on, lover boy. Activate your shield and, let's go kill Jevio."

Finn disappeared from sight and worry filled him. *Maybe this isn't a good idea.*

"Crow." Leslie smacked his side. "Come on."

He followed orders and kept a hold of her as they left the ship, making a beeline for the large estate. He felt Parker and Brisco's hands on his back.

The patrols went fast, unable to see the invading forces before it was too late. One moment, they were walking the perimeter, and the next, they were dead on the ground.

Crow knew groups were going to the guard towers to take out the pulse cannons and other defensives, but Crow and the others went straight through the front doors.

By the time they had searched the first floor, guards and slaves were rushing around, very aware of the attack.

"What the hell am I paying you for? They're already on the grounds!" The angry voice was very familiar to Crow. He'd scoured the media for every picture and videoclip he could find of Philip Jevio. "Get me to the fucking shuttle."

Crow darted up the stairs, following the loud voice. He felt Leslie's hand on his back as she ran with him.

Philip Jevio was still buttoning his pants as he left one of the rooms on the second floor. He was surrounded by security guards. "Bring the boy too. I'm not finished with his ass yet."

Two of the guards went back into the room, and Crow could hear sobbing.

He didn't think too hard, just stood at the top of the stairs and raised his phaser. One shot to the head and Philip Jevio was dead. The idiot hadn't even thought to shield himself during an attack.

For a moment, time seemed to stand still. Crow stared at Philip's dead eyes, and the security guards did the same.

Then, someone moved forward, vibroblade cutting through the guards' shields. They killed three before

Crow was able to shake off his paralysis. He fired again, focusing on one guard close to him, shooting him until his shield failed and Crow could fire the killing shot.

More came running, and Crow started to worry.

"Aww, someone already killed the bastard." Crow grinned when he heard Moyra's voice.

He put his phasers up and drew a short blade. He was better with a phaser but didn't want to take the chance of hitting one of the Charybdis Station soldiers. The large group of guards blocking the hallway made the fighting close, so Crow and the others deactivated their shields for visibility.

After that, the fight went fast. He jumped in, cutting into one of the guards and spinning the man around.

Moyra grabbed the wounded soldier. "Thanks, Crow." She shoved a frag grenade down the man's pants and pushed him toward the other guards.

Crow hid his face, trying not to vomit when body parts went everywhere.

"Damn it, Moyra." Leslie cut down another guard. "I think I have someone's guts in my hair."

Moyra just laughed and slid through the mess, running after the retreating guards.

Crow was about to follow, then remembered Jevio saying something about a boy. He opened the door Jevio had come from.

A shot hit his shoulder, but his shield held. He pushed forward and sliced into one of the two guards in the room. Brisco followed behind him, quickly taking out the second guard while Parker searched the rest of the room.

Once both men lay dead on the ground, Crow looked around. A huddled figure was curled up on the floor next to a bed. The young Cardinal-Wello hybrid looked to be in his late teens. He was naked and covered in bruises and *fluids*.

Crow scowled, happy he had killed Jevio. *Poor kid.* "Hey." Crow struggled to find something to say. "Jevio is dead. You're free now."

The young man looked up, grey ears twitching. "He's dead?"

"Yeah. Are you one of the slaves from Vextonar?" Parker asked, eyes softening. "We came to rescue you all."

The young man's eyes darted to the side. "Yes. I'm one of them."

Crow sighed. "You don't have to lie. Tell the truth, please."

Despair filled the man's face. "No. I'm not with them. I usually work in the kitchen, but Master Philip…" The young man shuddered. "Please let me go anyway. I swear I won't tell anyone."

Crow shook his head. "We came for the Vextonians, but all slaves owned by Jevio are free. You're good now."

The young man stood, legs wobbling. The hope in his eyes almost killed Crow. "Promise?"

"Yes." Crow forced the word out between clenched teeth. "Stay here until the fighting is over, okay? We'll come back for you."

"No! Please don't leave me." The man grabbed a sheet and wrapped it around his body. "I'll come too."

Parker tilted his head, eyes unfocused. "That was Ignali on my comm. The estate has been taken. Fighting is still going on downstairs, but the rest of the house is clear. We should stay here until it's finished."

The slave limped toward them. "Good. I'll stay with you two. All the slaves are free now?"

Brisco smiled. "Yeah. I'm Brisco. This is Parker, and this is Crow."

"My name is Lumi." The young man leaned against the wall. "I can't believe this is happening. We heard things, even isolated from the rest of the moon. We heard slaves were being freed."

"How long have you been a slave?" Parker asked.

"My whole life." Lumi swallowed. "Jevio owned my mom and dad too. They're gone now though."

The door pushed open, and Finn ran in, eyes searching the room until they landed on Crow. "You're covered in blood."

Lumi squeaked and darted behind Parker when Leslie and a few other Charybdis Station soldiers came in.

Crow gave Finn a slow smile. "It's not my blood. I wasn't injured at all."

Leslie whistled. "Not a single bit, Finn. Looks like you have some dancing to do."

Crow stayed by Finn's side as the fighting wrapped up. Lumi and three of the other slaves stayed right at their backs, huddled close together.

Finn smiled nervously. "Uh, Lumi? You and your

friends can pack your bags and wait in the shuttle if you want. We're going to be here awhile."

Lumi shook his head, and the young man and woman behind him did the same. "Cook is packing for us, not that there's much. We're staying right here. You can't leave us if we're with you."

Crow exchanged a look with Finn. "You can stay with us."

It took time, but eventually, they got back to the spaceport in Pagent's Distillery. Dermot, Jenise, and Crow's mom waited for them at the Blue Albatross's dock.

In a little over a week, Diana had changed drastically. Her hair was clean and styled in tiny braids that fell to her shoulders. Gone were her usual dress pants, and now she wore clothes very similar to his own – plain black pants and a black jacket of thin and tough material.

Diana's hard eyes met his. "Is he dead?"

Crow nodded. "It's over."

inn was exhausted. The last few days of processing the newly freed Vextonians and Jevio's slaves had been hell. They had recovered a little over half a million Vextonians and countless other slaves owned by the Jevio family.

Then there was Crow's family. Diana had taken the news of Jevio's death stoically. It was almost as if she didn't know how to react. Dermot had surprised them all when he'd broken down. Crow had needed to spend some time with them, and Finn was stuck on the Blue Albatross, writing reports with Weber, Halli, and Moyra.

Finn rubbed his eyes and leaned back in his chair. They still had so many Vextonians to find. He looked up and met Roxy's glowing eyes. She was wedged on top of one of the shelves behind his desk. His glimmer had likely spent most of her life in a crate, so she was only now stretching her wings and learning to fly.

"Meow." She sounded pitiful.

"Are you stuck up there?" Finn asked.

"Meow."

"I'll get her down." Moyra jumped up and pushed a chair over to the shelf.

"The Yellow General said Vextonar is still in turmoil," Weber said, drawing Finn's attention. The captain looked just as tired as Finn. "Leslie and Jada have offered ships to bring the Vextonians back to Charybdis Station for now."

"I'm glad Derelict, Beton, and Siletus have stepped up to help the other Vextonians. Charybdis Station has to be getting crowded, and the Boral System is closer to Vextonar," Halli said, stretching her arms over her head and grinning. "All together, we've recovered over a billion, guys. We've located, rescued, and began transporting over a billion people in a month."

Finn grinned. "We have, haven't we?" *With a lot of help from the rest of the galaxy*. It still shocked Finn when he thought of how the various planets had worked together to help them with the Vextonians.

"We'll find the others." Weber ran his hands through his hair. "I know we will."

Finn's grin faded. "Are we sure Ezvin wasn't in this group? Ival and his wife are a mess."

Halli sighed. "No. We triple checked."

Moyra huffed at Roxy's weight, then climbed off her chair and set the glimmer on the floor. Roxy instantly got a running start and flapped her feathery wings, lifting into the air. She flew back to the top of the shelf.

"Damn it." Moyra glared at the glimmer.

The door opened and Berenna walked in. A few of the freed Vextonians had chosen to stay on the Blue Albatross as they searched for the others. Berenna was one of them.

She gave him a tentative look. "Lieutenant?"

Finn went to her. "I'm sorry, Berry. He's not there."

She swallowed and smiled sadly. "Ignali already told me. I need to talk to Ival, and I wanted to know if you would sit with me. I know we don't know each other well, but I don't want to do this alone."

Finn nodded and took her hands in his, squeezing them lightly. "Sure thing. Can you come by my office in a couple of hours? We'll call him then."

She gave him a grateful look. "Thank you. I know you have so much to do. I really appreciate this."

"It's not a problem."

Berenna left, and Finn went back to his seat. "Are we sure Ezvin wasn't there?"

Weber gave him a sad look. "I'll check again."

Finn rubbed his face. "I know he's not there. Ival and Berenna's situation sticks with me for some reason. Ival is stuck on Genarg and can't come here, and Berenna is recovering from abduction, forced separation from her family, isolation, and months of being raped by fucking Verulo Malone. I wish would go to Charybdis Station so she could at least get counseling as she waits for Ival."

Moyra snarled. "Are you sure I can't cut Verulo Malone's dick off?"

"Not yet, Moyra. We need to make sure we've gotten all the information we can from him." After they left Rueal, Finn didn't particular care if the asshole had an *accident*.

Weber leaned over and squeezed his arm. "We're getting Berenna counseling while she's with us. I talked to my medical officer, and they check on her daily. She has her own quarters here and is close by as we search for Ezvin. We'll do our best by Berenna and so will you. We'll find Ezvin."

Finn raised his tablet and pulled up the child's picture again. He was only three when he was taken. By now, he would have turned four. "We will."

"Lieutenant." Ignali's voice came from the wall comm.

"Yes?"

"There's a handsome smuggler headed your way."

Finn pushed his tablet away and stood. "I, uh, have important things to discuss with Aiden."

"We'll pretend to believe you." Weber arched a brow. "We all need a break. What about meeting back here in an hour to continue?"

"Yes." Halli rubbed her eyes. "I need coffee and food."

Moyra huffed. "I need to go haunt someone. Maybe I'll sneak up on Noe. He's been in a foul mood for months."

Finn winced. *Poor Noe.* The Full Moon operative was the lieutenant of Moyra's ship. He had stepped in when Wolfe had decided to stay home for this mission.

The door to his office slid open and Crow stalked in, eyes focusing on Finn. They really hadn't seen enough of each other the last few days.

Finn stood and Crow picked him up, tossing him over his shoulder and heading for the door to Finn's quarters.

"Be back in an hour," Weber called out, laughing.

Finn stroked a hand down Crow's back and let his mate carry him into the bedroom. Crow stopped once the door closed behind them and let Finn slowly slide down his front. Crow tightened his arms around him and buried his face against Finn's neck.

"Mom is taking over my business," Crow said wryly. "Lumi and his two friends live in the villa now too. She spoils them rotten and put them to work sorting goods in the warehouses."

Finn snorted. "She needed something to do."

"She does it better than me." Crow sounded pitiful. "My contacts like her better, and she's the best haggler I've ever met."

Finn rubbed his back. "She can't help being efficient and charming. Where do you think you got it from?"

Crow sighed. "I guess I can't begrudge it for her. She's more like her old self since she moved into the villa."

"How's Dermot?"

Crow squeezed him, then set him on his feet. "Better. I don't think he dealt with Dad's death as well as I thought. It helped to know Jevio and Teresa Malone are both dead. Jenise said it was eating at him."

Finn nibbled his lip. "I wish he had talked to you. Then again, you didn't talk to him. I'm starting to think that the Crow men are a little too hardheaded."

"That is a good possibility." Crow nodded. He looked around. "Where's Hiss Beast?"

Finn pinched Crow's side. "Her name is Roxy. She's currently lurking on my office shelves."

Crow smiled softly. "She started flying?"

"Yes." Finn grinned, feeling proud. "Her wings have gotten bigger, and it's just been a week."

Crow sat on the sofa and pulled Finn onto his lap. "Brisco reported back on the Weasel."

Finn's ears twitched. "Really? Gus and Draif haven't been able to find much."

"Rumor has it the Weasel is a human hybrid and related to one of the aristocratic Rueal families. Brisco hasn't been able to find his base, but I have a hunch who might know." Crow kissed his neck. "Do you want to come along and have chat with Verulo Malone?"

Finn's tail swished back and forth against Crow's leg. "Why yes, I would enjoy that. Thank you for asking. We haven't been on a date in a while."

"It's important to keep our relationship fresh." Crow helped him stand. "Let's go interrogate a whiny, privileged, formerly rich man."

Finn kissed his cheek. "You have the most romantic ideas."

———

FINN STARED AT THE SLENDER, GREASY LOOKING MAN across the table from him and Crow. It would be so easy to stab his fork into Verulo Malone's eye. Crow took his hand, and Finn wondered if his expression had given him away. They sat in a simple diner in Pagent's Distillery. The city was slowly starting to come back to life. Thousands arrived every day and went back to their broken homes and businesses.

Finn forced himself to focus on the piece of shit in front of him. Verulo Malone may not be rotting in a cell, but he was now in a prison of his own making. Finn had confiscated every last credit of the Malone estate in the name of Charybdis Station and passed it on to a distant cousin of the Malone family.

Jada and the senate had approved, and now Verulo was completely destitute. Any friends he had thought he had were long gone, and no one on the planet would loan him credits.

Finn didn't feel an ounce of pity for the man.

Verulo leaned forward. "Are you buying?"

Crow smirked. "If you give us the information we need."

Verulo gave him a dark look. "I told that horrid banshee everything I knew about the fucking Vextonians."

"Not everything," Finn gently corrected. "There is one very large group we haven't been able to find any mention of, and Jada said you wouldn't talk about them."

Verulo sat back, a smug look on his face. "All I know is what was in Mother's notes."

"Strangely enough, they weren't mentioned there." Crow shrugged. "Somehow, about a million people just vanished."

"Weird." Verulo's eyes followed the waitress as she carried a tray of food to the table next to them.

Crow leaned on the table. "Tell us about your brother."

Verulo's attention snapped back to him, eyes narrowed. "Charybdis Station assassinated my brothers." He didn't sound too angry about the fact.

"Not Antonio and Raleigh." Finn picked up the menu and started looking over it. "We're talking about your brother the otter."

Verulo snorted. "It's the Weasel, and he's my cousin, not my brother."

Crow rubbed his chin. "So, he is a Malone."

Verulo flushed and slumped in his seat. "I don't know him. Mother never let him come to the estate."

"Where is his base?" Finn asked. "Hmm, this all looks good. You eat here before, Aiden?"

Crow stretched an arm around his shoulder. "Yeah. The burgers are great."

Verulo's stomach growled loud enough for Finn to hear over the noise in the busy diner. "I don't know."

"Bullshit." Crow didn't look up from the menu. "You hate the man. Why protect him?"

Finn looked up. "Do you think he'll help you?" Verulo's angry expression told Finn all he needed to know. "Ah, so you've already asked."

Verulo leaned forward. "Give me credits, and I'll tell you where his base is."

Finn tapped his chin. "Or, you tell us where the base is and we buy you dinner and don't kill you."

"*He'll* kill me if I don't get out of here." Verulo swallowed hard. "Give me enough to get off Rueal."

"Where you heading?" Crow asked.

"Not your business, hybrid," Verulo growled.

Finn sighed. "Okay, here's what I'll do. You tell us where the base is and one of Charybdis Station's ships will take you anywhere you want to go in the galaxy."

Verulo eyed him. "You'll buy me dinner too?"

Finn shrugged. "Sure."

"All I know is his base is on one of the moons surrounding Aruta. It's shielded well, and he works closely with the Belcrest assassins." Verulo looked around nervously. "When can I leave Rueal?"

Finn sent a message on his comm. "Let's order your meal, and Weber will come pick you up."

Verulo looked relieved. By the time Weber was there, Verulo's meal was ready and boxed up. "We're leaving right now?"

"Yes." Finn curled into Crow's side. "Weber will take you to one of our ships."

Weber grinned. "Let's get you somewhere safe, sir."

Crow frowned at Finn as the other two men left. "I don't like helping him. The first thing he'll do is warn the Weasel."

"He can't do that from a cell aboard Ronnie's ship."

Crow arched a brow. "What about giving him a ride to anywhere in the galaxy?"

"Oh, we will. We'll just wait to do it until after the Weasel is dealt with. Well, if he doesn't accidently die from a knife in his chest before then." Finn took a bite of his burger and chewed. "This really is good."

Crow shook his head and laughed. "You are something else, mate."

Finn grinned. "Now, tell me what you know about the Weasel. You said he was a pain in the ass."

"Yeah. He has a large fleet and attacks merchant ships. He also deals in slaves. He's known to board ships and take the crew and passengers to sell on the black auction."

Finn leaned back. "Black auction? Wait, Wyther said something about that. It's like a black market for slaves, right?"

Crow nodded. "They're harder to trace when they're sold through there."

"Do you think he's sold the Vextonians there?" Finn pushed his plate away, stomach gurgling.

"I don't know." Crow pulled him close. "The only way we'll know is if we take the base."

Finn leaned into him and typed out a message on his comm. "I'm sending Moyra's crew to scout Aruta's moons. We need to find him."

Crow waved the waitress over and packed their food up while Finn spoke with Moyra. By the time he was done, Crow had a bag of food. "Let's get you back to your ship."

Finn frowned. "I wish I could spend the night with you."

Crow cupped his face and leaned in for a kiss. "You are. I packed a bag."

———

FINN SAT WITH BERENNA IN HIS OFFICE WHILE CROW showered in their quarters. It really did feel like *their* quarters now.

Berenna took a big breath and let it out. "If this doesn't go well, can I join your mate's crew? I met Lumi yesterday, and he seems to like it."

Finn sat back in his seat. "You're welcome to if that's what you want, but isn't the plan to meet Ival at Vextonar? What's going on?"

She gave him an agonized look, then connected the call on the vid-screen in front of them. It didn't take long for Ival to pick up.

The large human's eyes went straight to his wife, and Finn could practically feel the longing the man felt. As usual, Ival's face took up most of the screen, and he looked like he was hiding in a closet or bathroom.

"Berenna. Damn, I'm happy to see you. Have you all found Ezvin yet? I think we'll be heading to Vextonar soon. Earth is going to lead a whole caravan of us there."

"We haven't found Ezvin yet." Berenna licked her lips. "I have something to tell you, but I can't bear for you to hate me."

Ival looked shocked. "I could never hate you, Renna. I love you."

"I'm pregnant," she said.

The silence lasted a while. Finn reached out and took Berenna's hand and watched the emotions play across Ival's face. Horror, sadness, anger, excitement. They were all there.

"What do you want to do?" Ival finally asked.

"I want to keep it," Berenna whispered, voice hoarse. "Dr. Walters told me it was a girl, and she's healthy."

Ival nodded, tears falling down his cheeks. "Then we're having a baby."

Berenna's stoic expression cracked, and Finn wrapped an arm around her shoulders as she started crying. "You don't hate me?"

Ival shook his head. "Never. I could never hate you. I, uh, should probably tell you my news too."

Berenna's tears slowed, and she leaned into Finn's side. "What are you talking about? You can't get pregnant."

Ival snorted. "You know how I came to Genarg when I couldn't find you and Ezvin?"

Berenna nodded. "You wanted to help kill the Crellic Queen."

Ival's shoulders slumped. "I thought you and Ezvin were gone forever. I didn't care if I lived or died."

"You lived." Finn gave him a pointed look. "You better not tell Berenna that you've remarried or some shit like that. I will fly across the galaxy and kick your ass."

Ival rolled his eyes. "I'm not married. As if I could move on knowing my mate was out there somewhere." He gave Berenna a guilty look. "I've made us a life here on Genarg. They need engineers like me, and I've helped with the planetary defenses. I also adopted two Crellic babies. They didn't have anyone, and I hated seeing them in the nursery all alone. Everyone in town took on some of the babies."

While Berenna watched the screen in amazement, Ival moved out of the closet he was in and walked through a cozy looking living room.

Ival turned his tablet, and Berenna and Finn saw two Crellic babies, both under a year old, in a playpen next to a sofa. The babies were large, but the Crells were pretty damn big. One of the babies had light green skin and the other was a pale blue. They each had tiny tusks in the corners of their mouths.

The green Crell saw Ival first and grinned. "Dada."

The little blue Crell giggled and held his arms up. "Dada."

Finn grinned at Berenna.

The woman was crying again, but this time the tears were clearly happy as she laughed. "Ival, you're a daddy again."

Ival reached down and picked up the blue baby. "I'll be a daddy to the little girl growing inside you too, Renna. Now, this here is our son Yavo and that's his sister Zelea. Earth helped me choose their names and told me they are traditional Crellic names."

Finn backed out of his office, leaving Berenna and Ival to talk. *I have to find Ezvin. He needs to meet his new brother and sisters.*

row watched Finn twist between the aerial silks in his quarters as soft and slow music filled the room.

Finn only wore a black lace thong and garter belt, and the black silks were a contrast against his tan skin. Currently, one leg was arched into the air, and the other was wrapped in silk. His strong arms held the silks, and he spun in a slow circle. Finn's ass teased him with each slow rotation.

Crow shifted in the chair, dick throbbing as Finn's body twisted and turned, displaying his firm muscles and smooth skin. Finn's tail swished in the air behind him as he moved.

This is literally the sexiest thing I've ever seen.

By the time the silk unrolled Finn to the floor, Crow was waiting on him. Finn's legs wrapped around Crow's waist as they kissed.

Crow's hands cupped Finn's bare ass, and he fell back on the bed. Finn moved to straddle him, arching his hips against Crow's and rubbing their cloth-covered dicks together.

They worked together to undress Crow, and a few minutes later, he slid into Finn's ass. His mate moved atop him, hands braced on Crow's chest, and he lifted, then slid back down, ass tightening around Crow's dick.

Finn rode him hard, groaning and shuddering each time Crow angled his hips to hit Finn's prostate. Finn's eyes rolled back and his ears twitched when he came, shooting seed all over their stomachs.

The contractions shivering through Finn's body were too much for Crow. He rolled Finn beneath him and pounded hard into Finn's ass, groaning when he came deep inside him.

When his body loosened, Crow fell against Finn, rolling to the side in an effort not to squash him. "That dance. You did it all the time on Cardinal's Hold?"

Finn panted. "Yeah."

Crow growled. "Fuckers saw you looking that sexy?"

Finn snorted. "I was even sexier then." He patted his soft stomach. "I've eaten too well the past twelve years."

Crow leaned over and kissed him, stroking a hand over Finn's belly. "You couldn't have been sexier. There's nothing more beautiful than you, Finn."

Finn rubbed his chin. "Now that you mention it, bellies *are* the epitome of sexiness. I mean, look at yours." He leaned over and pressed a kiss to Crow's stomach.

Crow laughed. "We're a pair, aren't we?"

"Yep." Finn leaned back against him. "We are."

Finn's wall comm chimed, and Ignali's voice interrupted them. "Lieutenant? Captain Wyther is calling."

"Put him through in my room." Finn rolled out of bed and pulled on a robe. Crow moved slower but donned his own robe and sat with Finn on the sofa in front of the vid-screen.

A moment later, Wyther's face appeared on the screen. "Lieutenant." The man's eyes widened, and he gave them a half smile. "Mr. Crow."

"What have you found out?" Finn asked, leaning forward. "You've read over my reports, right?"

"Yes." Wyther nodded. "I'm amazed how well everyone is doing. Unfortunately, the situation here isn't good."

"What's going on?"

"Mr. Crow's friend helped us get onto the planet, and he helped us locate the Vextonians. He even managed to get us a list and locations for them all. There are almost a million of them."

"Is he on there?" Finn asked. Neither Crow nor Wyther had to ask Finn who he meant.

Wyther shook his head. "No, Ezvin isn't here. I know you're disappointed, but he must be with another group. There are several other children in this bunch though. Most were sold as part of a group. Likely, their new owners see them as an investment."

"We need to get them out of there." Finn's ears lay flat. "What's the situation?"

Wyther winced. "The problem is the Vextonians are

all over the planet. They were sent here en masse, then sold. I don't know how we will possibly get them all without making our presence known."

Finn groaned and fell back in his seat. "I knew things were moving too fast. We were bound to come across a roadblock."

"Sneak in small groups and smuggle out the slaves?" Crow asked.

"I don't like that option." Finn's shoulders slumped. "It would take a while because we need to be thorough, and each ship we smuggle in and out increases our chances of being caught. If we're caught, there's a good chance Charybdis Station will end up at war with Dramacus."

"What about diplomacy?" Wyther asked. "Does the Lord Admiral have any sway with the planet?"

"None." Finn's eyes hardened. "The planet has cut off communication with everyone. Draif told me they have reached out to the planet but have had no response for months."

Wyther gave them an uneasy look. "There may be another option."

Crow arched a brow. Wyther looked like he had swallowed a bug. "What is it?"

"Dramacus may claim to have cut themselves off from the galaxy, but obviously, they're letting one type of merchant onto the planet."

"Slavers." Crow narrowed his eyes.

"What good does that do us?" Finn asked.

"It gives us a chance to get on planet and speak with officials in person." Wyther rubbed the side of his head.

"We can disguise one of our ships as a slaver ship and fill it with volunteers to look convincing, or we can find a willing slaver to help us get onto the planet."

Crow made a face. "Neither of those options are appealing. If we bring our own ship, we put everyone onboard in danger. One ship isn't enough to take a planet, and we have no idea how Dramacus officials will react. If we find a slaver willing to help, we can't truly trust them not to abandon us on the planet if things get difficult."

"My father is in the system." Wyther sighed. "I hate to ask him for anything, but I believe he will help."

"Why would he?" Finn asked. "I thought you were on really bad terms with your family?"

"Oh, I am." Wyther shrugged. "However, as much I hate the family business, we are still family. My father will help, and he won't abandon me on the planet."

"Okay." Finn nodded. "Let's say this works, and your father's ship gets us into the spaceport and in contact with officials. Why would they give us the Vextonians? It would be an expensive and complicated process even if we paid for each one to be recalled."

"That I can't help you with." Wyther looked thoughtful. "Well, one bit of gossip I've picked up is about the royal family. The population of Dramacus is varied. There are few purebred Dramiads in existence, and they all reside within the aristocratic families, and the royal family prides itself on its purity."

Crow tilted his head in thought. "I heard something a long while ago. A man I knew was trying to make some quick credits off Dramacus. He was marketing a drug designed specifically for the Dramiads."

Wyther nodded. "It was meant to cure Pleuli Feciose."

"What's that?" Finn asked.

Crow whistled low. "A disease that only effects Dramiads. It's a nasty one too."

"The man you're talking about was named Durgan Montrella," Wyther said. "He was executed as a public enemy of Dramacus when they discovered his *cure* didn't work. The royal family lost several members to the disease that year."

"So what does this have to do with us?" Finn asked. "I won't lie to the royal family and tell them we'll give them a cure for this disease in return for the Vextonians. That would be too cruel."

Wyther nodded. "I agree. However, Charybdis Station may not have a cure, but they do have some of the top medical research scientists in the galaxy."

Finn tapped his chin. "Alright. Contact your father, and I'll talk with the Lord Admiral. We'll meet again in the morning and hopefully come up with a plan."

"I'll call then." Wyther nodded and ended the call.

As soon as the vid-screen went black, Finn turned to him and crawled into his lap. "I have a feeling this is going to cost Charybdis Station."

"The royal family of Dramacus was never known for their pleasant personalities." Crow rubbed his cheek on Finn's hair. "We need to offer them something they desperately need. It doesn't have to be a cure for Pleuli Feciose, but it needs to be something

C.W. GRAY

big. Something that will make it worth the effort it will take to force their citizens to hand over the Vextonians."

Finn gave him a determined look. "We need to get to them, Aiden. I'll go in myself and pull each Vextonian out if I have to."

Crow patted Finn's thigh. "You need to make some calls. I'll head over to the villa and check on Mom and the others. I'll get Brisco to look into Montrella and see if his *cure* really was a scam or if he had some research behind it."

Finn clung to him a moment. "I know you're right, but I don't want you to go. I just want to go back to bed and snuggle, damn it."

Crow kissed him, hands stroking down Finn's back. "I want the same thing, love. I'll come back soon, and we'll get our snuggles in."

Finn nodded. "Okay. Take Roxy with you though. She needs some exercise, and I'll be in my office all day."

Crow eyed the glimmer. Roxy currently slept on a chair in the corner of the room. She looked all sweet and adorable, but Crow knew the hiss beast was a little terror.

"Aiden?" Finn's yellow eyes suddenly seemed to take up half his face. "You'll take her, right?"

Crow sighed. "Sure. It'll be fun."

———

CROW SAT IN ONE OF THE CHAIRS IN HIS OFFICE AND

134

watched his mom work at the desk. Since Diana had moved in, the room was far more organized and cleaner than it had been.

Roxy sat in his lap, cleaning her paws. Her wings were spread out and feathers tickled at his nose.

"This morning, we moved the last of the merchandise you bought last week." Diana looked up from her tablet. "I've filled the warehouses again though, so I'm going to need most of the crew with me. I'll let you have Parker and Brisco, mostly because they're your best friends, and I know they'll run off and help you anyway."

Crow grinned. "Mom, you've taken over my business."

"Well, you haven't been here, have you?" She arched a brow. "Not that it's a bad thing. If I would have known how fun this was, I would have worked with you a long time ago."

Crow laughed. "I can just imagine what Dad would have said to that."

Diana smiled sadly. "He would have been deliciously scandalized."

The ache in Crow's chest was a little easier to bear than it had been even a week ago. "Delicious?"

Diana laughed. "We would have argued, but then we would have had make-up sex. That's the best kind, Aiden."

Crow made a face. "I didn't need to hear you say that."

Her smiled faded, and she gave him a solemn look. "I'm glad you're here. I've been meaning to apologize to you. I wasn't there for you and Dermot like I should have been."

Crow shook his head and pet Roxy. "No, you don't, Mom. You were hurting. We get that."

She shook her head. "I'm hurting now too, Aiden. I'll always hurt. There will always be a Perick-shaped hole in my soul, and nothing will change that. That doesn't excuse the things I said to you. I lashed out at you and tried to hold you responsible for things you had no control over. You didn't start this mess on Rueal. The greedy-ass human purists did. Rueal has had problems for generations, and Humans First took advantage of that."

Crow felt his eyes water and pushed the tears away. His mom's words had hurt more than he had let himself admit. "I miss him so much, Mom. Dad always knew the right thing to do. I feel like I'm on the verge of fucking everything up all the time."

She leaned forward on her arms. "You know why you feel that way, don't you?"

Crow shook his head. "No."

"You have something to lose now. It's not just you and your crew making money." Diana smiled. "You have a mate, and because of him, you have a lot of people to save. The stakes are higher, son, and I know that's nerve wracking."

Crow rubbed his face. "Is this what love feels like?"

"Incredible and scary as hell?"

Crow nodded. "When I have Finn beside me, something settles deep inside. It's like if he's there, I'm whole. When he's gone, I'm thinking about when I can get back to him." He laughed. "Fuck, listen to me. Since when do I talk about how I feel?"

"Since you started feeling so much." Diana shook her head. "You and Dermot are just like me. I almost pity you boys." She was quiet a moment. "I want you to know I'll take care of your crew here. Even without Parker, I have this handled. You do what you need to and help your mate, even if that means moving to Charybdis Station."

His eyes widened. "What?"

She gave him a disbelieving look. "Your mate lives in a different system, baby boy. Haven't you thought of this?"

"Of course I have. I just thought you'd be mad if I considered it. I don't want to run from Rueal." He swallowed hard. "I don't want you to think I'm taking the easy way out."

She closed her eyes. "I'm an idiot, Aiden. I'm so sorry I've made you doubt yourself. You aren't tied to this damn planet. You've helped it more than I ever would have. Could you do more for it? Yes. Hell, I think Jada would love to polish you into a politician, but that's not you. Change is inevitable no matter what you decide to do. You could stay here and try to work with the senate to make Rueal a better place. You could also move to Charybdis Station and start a new chapter in your life. I'll miss you, but you have a new family to think of."

A soft knock on the door interrupted them, and Lumi opened the door to poke his head in. "Dinner is ready if you two want to eat."

Diana smiled kindly. "Thank you, Lumi. You know you don't have to cook for us, darling."

"I know." Lumi made a face. "I like cooking."

Diana smiled at Crow. "Come on, Aiden. Lumi cooks better than me."

Crow gasped dramatically. "Blasphemy."

13

*A*lmost a month later, Finn was still at a frustrated standstill. Moyra hadn't found the Weasel's base yet, and the Lord Admiral was still working on something for Dramacus. Fasi was being a little too mysterious for Finn's peace of mind. *At least Halli is continuing to make progress.*

Finn balanced on his silks, doing his best to focus his mind on holding the right position. Right now, he was hanging upside down between the two silks. Roxy perched on the bottom of his feet, adding her considerable weight to his own.

His door slid open, and Crow and Weber came in. The two men were talking and didn't notice Finn at first.

"Your friends have come in handy." Weber patted Crow's back. "We're moving the Vextonians far quicker than expected."

Finn smiled. Crow had given them the idea to use a relay system to move the Vextonians and the other freed slaves to their destinations. It had increased transportation times by fifty percent, and several friends of Crow's had offered to join in the relay.

"They were happy to help." Crow yawned, then looked around, eyes widening when they landed on Finn. "We interrupting your meditation, fluffball?"

Weber's eyes looked like they were about to pop out of his head. *You're just lucky I'm wearing leggings, Web.*

"Nope. I was about done."

Finn lifted one foot, and Roxy pushed off him. She flew around the room a couple of times, then landed on the bed. The glimmer curled up in the middle of the bed and closed her eyes.

Finn flipped and swung to one silk, then slid down to land on the floor. "Anything new to report?"

Weber closed his mouth and cleared his throat. "Uh, yes. Wyther's father arrived today, and Ignali received a message from the Blue Sparrow. Dru says she's bringing in a package for you and should arrive in the next hour."

"Dru?" Finn grinned. "I talked to Dannol last night, and he didn't say anything about Dru coming out. She must have left right after we talked to the Lord Admiral about Dramacus." He moved to cuddle into Crow's side. "I apologize in advance for anything Dru says. She's known me for a long time."

Weber snorted. "Plus, she has no filter."

Finn looked down at his workout clothes. "I'll shower and change before they get here. I wonder what this is all about. Maybe the Lord Admiral found something to offer Dramacus."

"We could use some progress." Weber rolled his shoulders and stretched his neck. "I'll see you all at the dock in an hour."

As soon as his friend was out the door, Finn pulled Crow down for a kiss. "Are you staying again tonight?"

Crow smiled against his lips. "Yes. Mom says I just get in the way at the villa."

Finn's head fell back as he laughed. "I really do love Diana."

Ignali's voice came from his comm. "Sir, there's a call for you from Charybdis Station."

"Thanks." Finn tugged Crow to the vid-screen and they sat down.

Fire appeared on the screen, Jellybean perched on his shoulder. The Element's cheek was puffed out, likely from cinnamon candies. "Hey, Finn. Is this your mate?"

Finn flushed. He hadn't managed to introduce Crow to any of his friends. "Yes. Fire, this is Aiden Crow."

Fire grinned. "Hey. I like your name. Leti gave me a book of Old Earth animals and it says crows are really smart."

Now it was Crow's turn to blush. "I've heard that."

Finn grinned and shoved another piece of cinnamon candy in his mouth. "Jellybean and I called to talk to Roxy. We have a story to tell her and some of the other pets want to meet her too."

Crow turned and gave him a baffled look.

Finn just smiled and nodded. *Like I understand the inner workings of Fire.* "Okay."

He didn't have to call Roxy. One moment she was sleeping and the next she clumsily flew across the room to land on the table in front of the vid-screen. "Meow."

"Hey, Roxy." Fire waved. "You remember Jellybean, right?"

Finn arched a brow. "Have you been calling my glimmer and talking to her, Fire? How would you even do that?"

Roxy gave him a lofty look. "Meow."

"He can't help it, Roxy." Fire made a face. "Ignore him. Now, here is Fluffle. She runs the neighborhood. You'll like her because she's tough, but fair."

Selene's cat stood up, paws braced on the vid-screen. "Meow."

"This is so strange," Crow whispered to Finn.

"This is Princess Buttercup," Fire said. Princess's scaly red head appeared over Fire's shoulder. "He has a lot of babies to take care of, just like Leti. Oh, Leti is his person. Sorry, I know this can get confusing."

Crow's eyes were wide. "Is that a Fire Veil dragon?"

Finn stood up. "We'll let you all talk. Nice to see you again, Fire."

Fire waved at him, smiling. "You too." He turned back to Roxy when Gravy appeared at Fire's side. "This is Gravy. He lives with Princess because his person is Hack, and Hack is mated to Leti."

Finn shook his head and tugged Crow away. "Let me shower and we'll go wait at the docks."

Crow snickered. "How often does he call to talk to Roxy?"

"I don't know." Finn sighed. "It's a good thing I love Fire."

An hour later, Finn and Crow stood with Weber and the other captains on the docks as Dru's ship landed. Finn wasn't sure what Dru had brought, but he was looking forward to showing Crow off to his friend.

The docking clamps locked onto the Blue Sparrow, and Finn tried not to bounce in place as he waited for the ramp to lower.

An excruciating number of minutes passed before the ramp finally lowered. Finn yelled and ran toward it when he saw a familiar face. "Amelia!"

The red-haired Cardinal raced down the ramp to meet him, hugging him tightly to her chest. "Oh, my Finn. Look at you! Where's your mate? I can't believe you didn't tell me you found him. I had to hear it from Ma Brackenstone. How do you think that makes me look?"

"Ma'am." Crow's deep voice came from behind them.

Amelia's eyes widened, and she smiled slyly. "Oh, Finn. You did well."

"Quit eyeing my man." Finn pinched her hip. "All that gorgeous perfection is mine."

Amelia arched a brow. "I saw how you practically swooned when you met. Maybe he needs a more mature woman."

Finn wrinkled his nose. "Who showed you?"

"It's all over the station." Amelia rolled her eyes. "You are ridiculous." She spun him around. "Let me chat with your mate while you see who else decided to come."

"What?" Finn looked back at Dru's ship, and his eyes widened at the sight of a large, purple Grell. "Lord Admiral? Who the hell let you off the station without an escort?"

Fasi groaned. "Renee and the boys have all yelled at me plenty. I am perfectly safe, and I have shit to do."

Dru and the rest of her crew stood around Fasi, eyes scanning the docks. There were quite a few more than usual, so at least they had added security.

Finn narrowed his eyes on Fasi. "What are you up to?"

Fasi sniffed. "Is that any way to greet your illustrious leader?" He pulled Finn into a hug. "We've missed you, son."

Dru poked Fasi's arm after a moment. "My turn." Her Vexal newt, Monty, perched on her shoulder.

Finn laughed when his friends passed him around, hugging him tightly each time.

Morgan and he hugged a little longer. "You still have her medallion?"

"It's in my pocket," Finn whispered. "I miss her."

"Me too."

Fasi patted his back. "Let's get onboard the Blue Albatross and meet with your captains." He waved his head toward the ramp. Death and his son Wyatt stood at the top. "We have something to offer Dramacus."

The two men had once looked very similar to one another. They were both a bit plain looking and of average height. At one time, they had shared their brown hair and eyes and tan skin. Now, though, Death was pale skinned with almost white hair and solid black eyes.

Wyatt though... Something was different. Finn's eyes stayed glued to Wyatt. "Morgan, is your mate pregnant?"

Morgan's grin lit up his face. "We just found out. How did you know?"

Wyatt leaned into his father's side and whispered something to him. The young man's skin practically glowed with happiness, and his hand rested on his abdomen.

"It wasn't hard to guess," Finn said wryly.

"Let's get to your big, fancy ship." Dru shoved him. "Amelia still has your mate."

Finn spun around, and sure enough, Amelia was still hanging on his mate's arm. "Amelia, I said you can't have him."

"We're just talking." She glared at him. "No one told me he has an older brother."

"Dermot is mated." Finn huffed. "Find your own mate."

Amelia just laughed at him and leaned up to whisper something in Crow's ear. Finn's mate laughed, then shot Finn a guilty look.

Finn grabbed Fasi's arm. "Let's go before Amelia steals my mate."

Soldiers surrounded Fasi, Wyatt, and Death as they made their way to Finn's larger ship. Fortunately, the Blue Albatross was close by, and the spaceport was still fairly empty.

Once they were all in Finn's office with his captains either in the room or on the vid-screen, Fasi spoke. "Our two Dr. Morricks believe they can make progress on curing Pleuli Feciose. Based on the research Mr. Crow sent us, we believe we saw where Montrella's scientists went wrong."

Finn took his normal seat in Crow's lap and focused on the conversation.

"They rushed things." Wyatt shook his head, a look of disgust on his face. "They focused on the symptoms rather than the actual disease. All he cared about was making it *appear* as if the disease were cured."

"With Charybdis Station's resources, we've already made progress," Death said. "We need information from the Dramiads to continue our research."

Fasi nodded. "We have something to offer them, Finn. We just need to get to them."

"We?" Dread followed his slow realization. "Fuck me, you can't come with us, Lord Admiral."

Fasi gave him a stubborn look. "I'm not asking. Dealing with Dramacus can potentially turn into a political nightmare. If a decision needs to be made for Charybdis Station, it will save time if I'm there."

"The royal family are narcissistic to the extreme." Crow gave Fasi a pained look. "I don't know that they will care about starting a war with Charybdis Station. You'd make a nice ransom payout."

Death patted Fasi's back. "I will ensure the Lord Admiral's safety."

Crow gave them all a disbelieving look. "I know the

stories going around and all, but one man can't take on a planet."

Finn leaned back and kissed Crow's cheek. "This one can." He turned back to Fasi. "Okay. You're the boss. How did you even get this past Renee, Draif, and the Council?"

Dru snorted, and Monty moved to perch on her head. "He didn't. The asshole showed up at my house and told me we were taking a short trip to Burnished Outpost."

Dru's lieutenant, Alois, shook his head. "We'll be going home to a bunch of unhappy people."

Fasi grinned and picked Finn up, hugging him tightly. "I wanted to meet your mate too. Mr. Crow has been very helpful in taking out Humans First, but Amelia and I need to make sure he's good enough for you."

Finn sighed and returned the big Grell's hug. "Wyther's father is already here. I guess the sooner we get this over with the better." Fasi put him back down, and Finn looked at Death and Wyatt. "Thank you for doing this. Dramacus has almost half of the missing Vextonians we've been searching for, including most of the children that were taken. This is going to make some families very happy."

Death nodded. "It is a small enough thing to do for so many. If the disease had been brought to my attention before, I believe I could have already created a vaccine."

"The royal family would have had to request it, and they're not ones to ask for help from outsiders,"

Wyther said. "The Montrella debacle has made them even more insular."

Finn rubbed his ears, trying to control his nervousness. Having Fasi with them both filled him with dread and made him happy. The man was his leader, but he was also a good friend. Fasi and Renee had welcomed Finn into their inner circle with open arms when he joined Hack's crew so many years ago.

"We'll leave in the morning," Fasi said, nodding. "Wyther, how many of us can your father bring in?"

"His ship will hold two hundred thousand slaves," Wyther said, voice full of disgust. "Those are tight quarters though. I suggest we bring a light crew and leave room to take some of the Vextonians with us. Two hundred thousand soldiers won't do us a bit of good anyway."

"Good point." Fasi rubbed his chin. "Me, Finn, Dru's crew, and Death and Wyatt should work."

"I'm going too." Crow nodded, eyes narrowed. "I go where my mate goes."

The air on either side of Fasi shimmered, and two Full Moon operatives appeared. Finn recognized Otto and Sandve.

"We'll be going as well," Otto said.

Sandve smiled at Finn. "Nice to see you again, Lieutenant."

Finn grinned. "Sandve!" He hugged the assassin. "I thought you went with Cas."

The tall Dedril smiled. "Bendix wanted to stretch his legs a bit, so he went instead. I promised to keep an eye on the Lord Admiral." He eyed Fasi. "I thought it was going to be an easy job."

"Sandve." Crow rolled the name around on his tongue, his expression showing his displeasure. "Why are your hands still on my mate? A friendly hug doesn't last that long."

Finn glared at Crow, but Sandve's eyes brightened, and he hugged Finn again. "Oh, your mate is going to be so much fun."

"He's a bit growly, but once you get to know him, he's a big softy." Finn stepped away from Sandve. "I should warn you that he's a good shot too. Just so you know." With the way Crow was glaring at Finn's friend, it was pertinent information.

Fasi wrapped an arm around Crow's shoulders. "Don't go getting jealous, son. Trust me, it's never the right response. Renee has kicked my ass more than once for not trusting her. Now, Finn told us all about your mom. Amelia and I would like to meet her and chat before we leave in the morning."

Crow continued to glare at Sandve until Fasi walked him out of the room.

"Why does he hate me?" Sandve asked.

"The better question is why *wouldn't* he hate you." Otto chuckled and shoved his friend. "You're annoying as hell."

"I'm a fucking angel." Sandve sniffed and shoved Otto back. "It has to be something else."

"Gee, what could it possibly be?" Dru tapped her chin. "You're handsome, an unknown friend of his new mate, and all touchy-feely with Finn. Hmm, I just can't understand it."

Lerais frowned at his wife. "Sandve isn't that handsome. His ears are too big."

Sandve glared at Lerais and covered his ears. "They're perfectly proportionate to my head."

Lerais nodded. "Now that you mention it, your head *is* pretty big."

———

THAT NIGHT, EVERYONE GATHERED AT THE VILLA, AND Diana, Amelia, and Fasi exchanged embarrassing stories about Finn and Crow.

Finn tugged on Crow's arm. "Let's go into the kitchen."

Crow was grinning, completely involved in the story Fasi was telling about Finn's first mission on the Blue Solace. "I need to hear this."

"They were only supposed to scare the man a little," Fasi said. "The point of the whole mission was to get him to agree to leave the colony alone, and a little fear goes a long way. It was going well, but then the man made a mistake – he tugged on Finn's tail."

Crow frowned, eyes narrowed. "Then they killed him, right? No one gets to touch my mate's tail but me."

Fasi chuckled. "They almost did. Hack got growly and set the man's house on fire, and Selene almost cut the man's hand off. Finn was so mad at everyone because he didn't get to do anything."

Dru leaned over from where she perched on

Lerais's lap and tweaked his ear. "Aww, we let you in on the next fight, didn't we?"

Finn crossed his arm and scowled. "It wasn't the same."

"Everyone's always protective of Finn." Amelia smiled softly. "I remember when one of our clients tried to talk him into bed. He was only fourteen at the time, and my kittens were pissed that the asshole was trying anything with our sweet little Finn."

Finn groaned. "I'm going to the kitchen." He left them in the front room and stalked past his captains playing poker with Parker, Brisco, and other members of Crow's crew.

Brisco raised his cup in a slightly drunken salute. "Lieutenant. Parker and me are comin' with you to the snooty royal people planet."

Finn rolled his eyes. "Maybe you shouldn't drink more until after dinner."

Brisco pouted. "Why are you so mean?"

Finn found Lumi in the kitchen humming a song and bustling around happily. The former slave had practically shouted with joy at the chance to feed a crowd. Berenna sat at the table, chatting to Ival on her tablet.

"Lumi, what can I do to help?"

Lumi eyed him. "I've heard about your cooking abilities. Here, cut these vegetables." Lumi put a huge bowl of a variety of native Rueal vegetables in front of him. "Did you really set your ship on fire trying to cook like Dru said?"

Finn growled. "Everyone's telling my business."

Lumi arched a brow.

"Yes." Finn flushed. "I did set the Blue Solace on fire, but Hack does it all the time."

Lumi gave him a sympathetic look. "How do you feed yourself?"

Finn wrinkled his nose but went to work chopping. "I rely way too much on my friend Juniper. He has a diner on Charybdis Station and most of the crew goes there to eat."

Lumi looked over his shoulder. "Do you miss your home?"

"Yes. It's nice to see Dru and the others here." Finn blinked away tears. "It's stupid, really. It's just been a little under three months since I've seen everyone, but I got used to being with my friends all the time. I was about your age when I moved to Charybdis Station and met my best friend, Dannol. It's been home ever since."

"Do you think you and Crow will move there when this is all over?" Lumi asked softly.

Finn shook his head. "No. I'm going to talk to the Lord Admiral sometime soon and tell him I'll be moving here. This is Aiden's home, and Diana and Dermot live here. They all need each other." He swallowed back the lump in his throat. "It'll be hard, but he's my mate. I'll be happy as long as I'm with him."

Lumi looked thoughtful. "I never had a home before Diana took us in. I like it here, Finn, and I can tell you that Diana doesn't *need* either of her sons. She can stand on her own."

"They're family." Finn shook his head. Lumi didn't understand the connection the three shared.

Diana poked her head into the kitchen. "Finn, I think I'm in love with Amelia. I'm keeping her, alright?"

Finn shrugged. "I guess you can, but she's handsy so keep her away from Aiden."

Diana laughed and disappeared.

Finn's comm chimed, and he set the knife down and wiped his hands on a towel before answering. Moyra's grinning face projected above the small device strapped to his wrist.

"Give me good news." Finn bounced on the balls of his feet and pulled Hazel's medallion from his pocket.

"We found the base." She wiggled her brows. "It was very well hidden. They don't have our tech, but their own is pretty impressive. We passed by it several times. The fourth time around, Noe noticed a shimmer and went to check it out. The fucker takes up almost half of the smallest moon around Aruta. He has an atmospheric shield, housing, warehouses, and a spaceport all his own."

"Can you get in to scout it?"

"We're working on it. Alber is trying to crack their defensives without being seen, but it will take some time."

"Be careful." Finn gave her a hard look. "We kinda like you and the others, so don't get yourselves killed. Gather as much information as you can, then come back to Rueal and start planning with Weber and the other captains. I'll be dealing with Dramacus for the next few weeks."

"Weber updated me." Moyra blew out a breath. "Do you think it will work? That's a lot of slaves to hand over and most of them don't belong to the royal family. They'll be pissing off quite a few of their citizens."

"It's the best plan we have." Finn nibbled on his lip. "At least Death will be with us."

"True. That is one scary fucker." Moyra gave him a sly look. "Did Val come too or is Morrick all alone?"

"Just Wyatt came with." Finn gave her a suspicious look. "Why?"

"Full Moon has a bet going about how long it will take Death and Val to admit they're mated. Everyone knows it, but it took forever for them to even go public with their relationship."

"Is it really our business?" Finn asked, snorting.

"Of course not." Moyra rolled her eyes. "That's what makes it fun."

14

SUGARWORM SYSTEM, EN ROUTE TO PLANET DRAMACUS

*A*fter a week of being onboard the large slaver ship, Crow was more than ready to get the hell away from it. The place was designed to hold multiple people against their will as they traveled from one location to another. It was creepy and disturbing as hell. At least it only had a few crew members onboard for this trip. Dru's ship took up some space in the cargo bay.

Then there was Wyther and his father. The icy tension between the two men was almost palpable.

At the moment, Crow sat with Fasi in a small cubby. He had been surprised at how well he got along with Charybdis Station's leader. It should have been intimidating to speak with the Grell, but Crow found himself at ease around Fasi. He reminded Crow of his dad in a lot of ways.

"More than fighting wars goes into running a station, and I could use a good person in the economic division. You have contacts across the galaxy that we don't, and I think you'd be an asset to the station." Fasi watched him carefully, eyes sly. "You could even help establish a trade route between the station and Rueal."

Crow grinned. "Stop trying to bribe me to move to the station."

Fasi laughed, deep and loud. Nothing about the man was quiet or unremarkable. "I can't help it. I don't want to lose Finn, and I know he'll follow you all around the galaxy."

Crow shrugged and bit his lip. "We haven't talked about what will happen when this is over. I know he's happy on Charybdis Station. I'll miss my mom and brother, but I won't separate him from his home."

Fasi gripped his shoulder. "He wouldn't want to separate you from your family either. You two need to talk about this and find a solution that works for both of you."

Crow sighed. "We do, especially now."

Fasi tilted his head. "What's that mean?"

Crow looked around for a minute, then undid his jacket and lifted his shirt. His birthing line was usually barely visible against his dark skin. Now, though, the edges were a dark pink. So far, Finn hadn't noticed it, but they had mostly been snuggling at night instead of their normal naked workout.

Fasi whooped and slapped his knee. "I should have known. The Blue Solace men work fast, you know. Stay here. I'm going to go get Wyatt to give you a scan and make sure everything is okay."

Crow blinked, still holding his shirt up in the empty cubby. He hadn't known Fasi could move that fast. He was still sitting like that when Fasi returned with a baffled Wyatt.

The doctor looked half asleep. "I was napping."

Fasi hugged Wyatt, then pushed him closer to Crow and handed him his scanner. "Go ahead and scan him. Tell me there's a little Finn in there."

Wyatt shook his head and gave Crow a wry look. "Sorry. Fasi gets excited about the babies." He held his scanner up and ran it over Crow's body, then took a sample of his blood. "Give me a minute, and I'll let you know."

Crow let his shirt fall back down. "I'm not sure if I *want* to know. A kid wasn't something I was planning on anytime soon."

Fasi gave him a solemn look. "How are you feeling?"

Crow swallowed and rubbed a hand over the top of his head, noting he'd need a haircut soon or his curls would get out of hand. "Scared? Excited? Maybe a little in love with the idea. Can you imagine a tiny Finn crawling around? That would be the cutest damn thing in the galaxy. Do they make diapers with holes for tails? They would have to, right?"

Wyatt looked up from his scanner. "Okay. You are pregnant. It's early, maybe two weeks."

Crow's vision dimmed for a minute before clearing. "Shit, it's real."

Fasi wrapped an arm around him, and Wyatt settled a hand on his shoulder. "Whatever you and Finn decide, you two aren't alone," Fasi said. "Even if you stay on Rueal, I have a long reach and need to take more vacations."

Crow licked his dry lips. "You are the strangest planetary leader I know."

"That's the truth." Wyatt giggled. "He's too damn kind and giving to have been a mercenary leader less than five years ago."

The comm on the wall flashed, drawing their attention. "We'll land on Dramacus within the next hour."

Fasi's eyes widened. "I thought we were farther away."

"Meet in Old Wyther's office?" Crow asked.

"You really need to stop calling him Old Wyther." Fasi snickered. "Old *and* Young Wythers don't like it."

They walked together to Degran Wyther's office. Wyatt moved to stand between Death and Morgan as soon as they arrived.

Degran nodded to them. "We're approaching the planet now. We didn't expect to get into the spaceport so quickly. Usually, we have to wait a day or two before they let us land."

"What's the plan?" Finn asked. "We've talked about what we'll do when we make contact, but how are we going to get in front of the royal family?"

"I've contacted the steward at the palace and told him I have a special package for the king. In the past, I've brought specialty slaves directly to the king and queen." Degran winced. "I hope this works, because if it doesn't, I'll lose a damn profitable customer."

"What a shame," Wyther said dryly.

Degran glared at him. "Naiene will meet us at the dock."

"Thank you, Degran." Fasi nodded. "We may not approve of your profession, but we do appreciate your help."

Degran shrugged. "You're paying, so there's that. I can always use credits."

Crow hid a smile. They *were* paying Degran, but the amount was tiny when compared to what the man would have been making if he wasn't wasting his time carrying them around the system. Crow thought the man cared more about his son than either of them realized.

Finn wiggled under Crow's arm and snuggled against his side. "You were gone when I woke up," he whispered. "Roxy and I didn't get our morning snuggles."

"Sorry. I was having a chat with Fasi."

Finn nipped Crow's arm. "He better not have been telling stories about me again."

Crow leaned down and kissed Finn. He loved hearing tales about his mate and all the people on Charybdis Station. He really needed to meet Dannol. Somehow, Crow hadn't managed to be there during any of Finn and Dannol's many conversations via vid-screen.

Thirty minutes later, they all stood at the ramp of Degran's ship.

A dark-skinned Dedril hybrid with bright yellow scales lining his brown face met them on the dock. Naiene went straight to Degran and hugged the man. "We thought you'd given up your business, old friend.

From what the others tell me, it's been over a year since you attended any auctions."

Wyther's eyes flew to his father. "What?"

Degran flushed and cleared his throat. "This isn't a normal visit, Naiene. I'm not here to sell any merchandise. This is Lord Admiral Fasi Juren from Charybdis Station, and he has one hell of an offer for King Xaran."

Naiene's eyes widened. "Charybdis Station? Our planet wants nothing from you, Lord Admiral." He shook his head. "Degran, this is unexpected."

Degran held his hand up. "The king will want to hear this. I swear to you, this is a good deal for Dramacus."

Naiene looked conflicted for a moment. "Stay here. I'll see what I can do." He walked away and spoke into his comm.

"That could have gone worse," Morgan said, shrugging.

"Don't count yourself lucky yet." Degran looked uneasy. "Naiene could be calling enforcement."

Wyther moved to stand next to his father. "What's this about you not dealing in slaves for over a year?"

Degran sniffed. "Slaves aren't as profitable anymore. I've been moving medical equipment and other goods. The pay is better, and you don't have to feed inanimate objects."

"Bullshit." Wyther shook his head. Crow had never seen the man so angry. "There is nothing more profitable than slaves."

Degran glared at Wyther. "Maybe we don't want to

deal with the trouble anymore. Your brothers are brokering deals with planets that don't deal with slavery, and your mom and I are wanting to retire. It's a good move, but it ain't any of your business. You don't want nothing to do with us, remember?"

Wyther closed his eyes and took a deep breath. "We've had this conversation before, Dad. I still love you, mom, and my idiot brothers, but I won't be a part of selling other people. I've seen firsthand how horrible it can be."

Crow and Finn exchanged a look. This was getting personal, and Crow wished they could give Wyther and Degran some space.

"It's just business." Degran scowled. "You never let us talk to our grandkids. You just send pictures."

"We don't want them thinking slavery is something that is normal or acceptable." Wyther's own expression echoed his father's. "We won't compromise on that."

Neiene returned, interrupting their discussion. "King Xaran has agreed to meet with you, Lord Admiral. He has one hour to spare, then you are to return to your ship and leave." He turned to Degran. "You are not to return again. I'm sorry."

Degran sighed. "I understand. Thank you, Neiene."

Crow held Finn's hand as they followed Neiene through the spaceport. They were met with a large group of guards, but Crow couldn't say that was too unexpected.

He was selfishly thankful Wyther and Degran's issues were distracting him from his own worries. Crow couldn't fathom what Wyther was going through. He loved his mom and brother, but if they were involved in the slave market, it would be hard to respect or trust them.

They were quickly transported from the spaceport to the palace. Crow was used to seeing opulence on the estates of the aristocrats of Rueal, but the palace of Dramacus put them all to shame. The rest of the city wasn't in shambles, by any means, but it was clear where the wealth was centered.

The spacious grounds were sculpted perfection, and the glowing, light blue walls of the expansive structures glittered in the sunshine.

Their transports came to a stop, and they all unloaded and gathered around Fasi. Sweat trickled down Crow's spine. *Shit can go so wrong here.*

Brisco and Parker pushed close behind him.

"Boss," Parker whispered. "There are guns aimed at us from above."

Crow looked up and noticed the armed guards stationed on the multiple levels of the many buildings. *I hope Death is as big a weapon as they say.*

They were led through halls filled with guards and finally came to a stop in a large meeting hall. King Xaran sat behind an intricately made desk. The surface was bare of tech and clearly meant more for presentation than actual function. The room was full of palace guards. They lined the wall and stood in rows behind the king's desk. It made for an imposing sight, and Crow fully understood why they were all allowed in to see the king. *We stand no chance of getting out of this if it comes to a fight.*

Crow's eyes caught on the king. He had met plenty of Dramiad hybrids on Rueal, but he had never met one of the pureblooded, though he had seen pictures in the media of the royal family.

In person, the pureblooded Dramiad king was impressive. His light green skin was lined with purple markings unique to him. As was typical for other Dramiads, he had no hair atop his head or on his face.

The king didn't rise as they entered, and even sitting, Crow noted he was damn tall. He estimated the king would be well over eight feet. Despite his height, the man was skeletally thin. His long, many layered robes tried to conceal it, but Crow didn't think that was normal of most pureblooded Dramiads. *But what the fuck do I know?*

Xaran didn't look pleased. "Lord Admiral, this is quite the surprise. Did my proclamations not make it clear that Dramacus wants absolutely nothing to do with planets outside our own?"

Fasi eyed the two slaves kneeling beside Xaran's desk. "Clearly, you want something from the rest of the galaxy."

Xaran arched a brow. "Did you truly go to all this trouble to lecture me on the wrongfulness of slavery?"

Fasi snorted. "If I thought it would do any good, I would have. No, we came for another reason. You purchased almost a million of the Vextonians Wineon sold into slavery." This time Fasi arched a brow. "Were my many messages not clear in stating if a person or institution didn't willingly hand them over, Charybdis Station would consider them an ally of Humans First?"

Xaran rolled his eyes. "I don't read messages sent by *any* planet, little less a floating metal island. We aren't handing anyone over. The Vextonians are legal property of my citizens now."

Fasi kept his face blank. "You truly don't want to be my enemy, Xaran. For the sake of your people, I am going to make you an offer so we can resolve this peacefully."

Xaran gave him a look of disbelief. "You come to *my* planet with a party of... What?" He counted the people standing behind Fasi. "Thirty-eight people. You come here with thirty-eight people and threaten me?"

Fasi shrugged. "That's no threat, just fact. Now, I'd like you to meet Dr. Verion Morrick and his son, Dr. Wyatt Morrick."

Xaran's eyes widened slightly. "Verion Morrick? The royal physicians have spoken highly of your research with genetic diseases." He licked his lips nervously. "There have been rumors of your death and... other things."

Death nodded. "As you can see, I am very much alive."

"Yes." Xaran turned to Fasi. "What is this all about?"

"Pleuli Feciose." The room went completely still at Fasi's words.

Xaran's face grew dark. "What do you know of it?"

"It's not a secret, Xaran. It's a disease that effects pureblooded Dramiads." Fasi sighed. "I personally didn't know anything about it until recently, but we've heard of the debacle Montrella caused by trying to con your people."

Xaran snarled. "We had hope for the first time in our history, and it was just a farce. Montrella was executed for his crimes. Keep that in mind, Grell."

Fasi nodded. "Verion and Wyatt have begun researching the disease. They need information and samples from pureblooded Dramiads before they can progress any further."

Xaran's face was emotionless. "You can cure it?"

Death shook his head. "I can't say that. I think Wyatt and I stand a good chance of it if we work together, but I won't make false promises."

"What do you want, Juren?" Xaran asked.

Fasi gave the king a hard look. "Each and every one of the Vextonians your people bought."

"That's impossible." Xaran shook his head. "They're private property."

"That's the only deal I'm willing to make." Fasi exchanged a look with Death. "If you want Charybdis Station's best to try to find the cure, then you will hand over the Vextonians. If you don't want to do this, then Verion will give you his notes and we'll leave. Your royal physicians can keep trying."

Xaran stood, smirking. "Or, I'll keep your scientist and his son, and they'll develop the cure or die." He waved toward the guards. "Grab the two doctors. Kill the rest."

Death smiled. "Bad idea."

Xaran glared. "Guards!"

Crow looked around the room. Every guard and Dramacus official was frozen in place, unmoving.

Some were in the process of stepping forward, and others had their weapons posed to attack.

Degran waved a hand in front of Neiene's face, and the man didn't move or acknowledge him. "What the hell?"

Death moved to stand in front of Fasi and faced Xaran. "I won't tolerate any threats against my friends and family, Dramiad. I am a citizen of Charybdis Station, and I will protect them with my life. As you can see, some of those rumors you've heard are correct. I can easily kill every last person on your planet if I wish, or I could freeze them in place and our people can take the Vextonians, one by one. We know who is here and where they are."

Xaran shook as he fell back in his seat. "What do you want?"

Death gave him a look. "I believe the Lord Admiral has already told you what we want. Since you are suffering from Pleuli Feciose yourself, I will try to forgive this slight of yours. This time."

"This is our last offer, Xaran." Fasi moved to stand beside Death. "Will you give us each of the Vextonians in exchange for Verion and Wyatt's help?"

Xaran stared at his frozen guards. "Fine."

Fasi nodded and smiled. "That wasn't so hard, was it? Transport ships are already on the way here to collect the Vextonians. I want them all by the end of the week. If you need a list of names and locations, we can get that for you. If any of them are harmed in any way... Well, do I even need to say it?"

Xaran shook his head.

"Wyatt and I will set up our stations on the Blue Sparrow within your spaceport and begin working. Please send at least twenty pureblooded Dramiads to our ship so we can collect samples," Death said. "If your physicians have any notes or samples of their own to share, it would be appreciated. Also, we would like files and blood and stool samples of any current cases they are treating, including yours. Wyatt and I will make this our primary focus and do the best we can to develop a cure, a vaccine, or both. At the moment, there are too many possibilities for me to provide you with a timeline. I'll update you on our progress daily."

Xaran nodded. "My guards?"

"They'll be fine once we're out of the palace." Death smiled again, and Xaran shuddered. "You're lucky I'm with Charybdis Station now. My Lord Admiral is far kinder than I am. I would have killed you by now and taken what I wanted. Your soul is in need of harvesting."

Crow looked at Finn. His mate seemed far too calm for this conversation.

Parker's hand on his back startled him. "Boss, this is some bizarre shit."

Sandve's voice came from behind him. "Yes, it is. I don't even know why I bothered coming."

Crow sniffed. "Me neither."

15

SUGARWORM SYSTEM, EN ROUTE TO PLANET RUEAL

A few days later, Degran's ship was full of Vextonians. Finn and the others were lounging in the commons with Fasi and his guards. While Dru and her crew had stayed behind with Death and Wyatt, the bulk of the soldiers had gone with Fasi.

"You weren't scared at all, were you?" Crow asked for the hundredth time.

Finn groaned and snuggled into his mate's side, contemplating the cards in his hand. "No, I wasn't. I've seen Death in action. He has some wild powers. I'm glad too. We'll get each and every slave back without casualties of our own and within a short time. That's a win, Aiden."

"Yeah, Aiden." Sandve studied his own cards before drawing another. Roxy hissed from her own chair next to Sandve, and the operative jumped. "Damn brat."

Crow stroked the glimmer's head. "Good girl."

Finn looked across the mess hall. "Look." A Vextonian child was curled up on Fasi's lap, staring at the Lord Admiral's tablet as he talked to his mom and dad. "We may not have found Ezvin yet, but we've still saved quite a few today.

Crow's face softened. "Yeah. It's a big win."

Brisco sat at the table, tablet held in front of him. On the screen, Finn could see Death. The man sighed heavily. "What do you want now?"

Brisco grinned. "What does my soul look like now? Is it better? I helped clean all the toilets on the ship. By the goddess, that had to have made my soul all shiny, right?"

"Why aren't you afraid?" Death almost sounded plaintive. "You should be. You're irritating the hell out of me."

"Sorry, Dr. Morrick," Finn said and reached over to turn off Brisco's tablet.

Crow's friend glared at him. "What the hell, Finn?"

Sandve shook his head and dealt another round of cards. "Your friends have no common sense, Aiden."

Finn thought that maybe Sandve didn't have much common sense. He seemed to take great joy in baiting Crow.

Parker slid into a seat at their table. "Remember, boss. He's your mate's friend, so you can't kill him. Also, he's too fast for me to shoot."

Sandve grinned. "Aww, I like you too, Parker."

Parker rolled his eyes. "Anyway, Brisco and I are going to Charybdis Station with you guys when this is over."

Finn raised his brows. "What makes you think we're going to Charybdis Station when we have all the

Vextonians? Aiden has his family, a nice villa, and a business on Rueal."

Crow snorted. "I do have my family, but Mom took over the villa and my business."

Parker nodded. "She's better at it then he is too. She stays mostly legal to throw off the authorities and only smuggles out the really profitable stuff. Everyone trusts her 'cause she looks so damn sweet."

"Well, Jada knows." Crow grinned. "She grew up with me, so she knows Mom's ways."

Finn swallowed hard. "You're saying you'll move to Charybdis Station?"

Parker leaned over and kissed Finn's forehead. "Yes, sweetheart. I'll move to Charybdis Station."

Sandve started shaking with laughter. "I really do like you, Parker."

Crow growled and swatted at his friend. "Get out of here."

Parker laughed and leaned into Brisco. The other man had Death on his tablet again. "What about my soul, Morrick?" Parker asked. "Is it black as the night sky?"

Finn ignored the people around them and turned to his mate. "Are you serious about this, Aiden? We haven't talked about it."

In fact, they had gone out of their way to avoid talking about it. They had spoken about all kinds of things – their pasts, their friends and families, their hopes for the future – but they hadn't discussed where that future would be.

Crow looked around for a moment, then jumped

up, keeping Finn in his arms. "Let's go to our room. It's too crowded here. Sandve, babysit Roxy."

Sandve scowled. "Damn it."

Finn let Crow carry him down the hall. Their *room* was a glorified broom closet with no windows. *Fuck, I'm become a pampered officer.*

When the door shut behind them, Crow set him down. "Okay, so I spoke to Fasi about work on the station. Mom already gave me her blessing, and I'll talk to Dermot when we get back home."

"Home." Finn took Crow's hands. "Rueal is your home. I don't mind moving there. I won't lie. It'll be hard to leave Charybdis Station, but you're my mate, Aiden, and I love you. Our mating has been a bit of a wild ride because of my duties, but *you're* my home, not the station. As long as I'm with you, I'll be okay."

Crow cupped his cheek and stroked a thumb across Finn's lips. "You don't see the way you light up when you talk about Dannol and the others. When you left Cardinal's Hold, did you miss it as much as you would miss Charybdis Station?"

Finn winced. "I missed Amelia, but you're right. Cardinal's Hold was never home."

"Charybdis Station is." Crow gave him a half smile. "Believe it or not, I'm excited to switch things up. Rueal will get back on its feet without me. Mom is having a good time with the business, and Dermot and Jenise will start their own family soon. I love you, Finn. I know I put off saying it, but I'm ready now. I want my chance with you."

Finn jumped, wrapping his legs around Crow's

waist when his mate caught him. Finn pulled him down for a kiss, hands shaking with emotion. "I want my chance with you too."

Crow laughed and took his time putting Finn back on his feet. "I kinda have some news for you."

Finn frowned. "Why aren't we on the bed now? That was the plan, right?"

Crow snorted. "We'll get there. Hold on, fluffball." He lifted his shirt, baring his abdomen. "We haven't gotten enough naked time lately, but I had Wyatt do a scan."

It took Finn a moment to figure out what Crow was saying. His eyes widened when he finally noticed Crow's birthing line. "Oh shit! A baby?"

Crow nodded, eyes nervous. "How do you feel about it? I'm scared shitless but excited too. I can see us with kids, but I always thought it would be a few years down the road."

Finn's heart was beating too fast, and his vision dimmed around the edges. He could see them with a couple of kids back home on Charybdis Station.

His house wasn't a villa, but it was nice, and Dannol was right next door. The kids could play with all the pets in the neighborhood, and they wouldn't lack for friends. Hell, Leti was probably pregnant again or had adopted another kid by now. It had been a whole two weeks since Finn had spoken with him.

"I can keep Dannol?" Finn asked, barely recognizing his voice. His fingers touched the tears coming from his eyes. "I didn't want to leave him, Aiden. I would for you, but he's my best friend, and I came so close to losing him like I did Hazel."

Crow hugged him tightly. "I'm sorry I didn't realize how much this has been weighing on you. I pretty much made up my mind a few weeks ago."

Finn buried his face in Crow's shoulder. "I didn't realize it either. I've been trying not to think about it. Can we have snuggle time? We've not had enough lately."

Crow looked surprised. "You want snuggle time instead of naked time?"

Finn chuckled. "Yes, but don't get used to it."

They unhooked their comms and took off their boots before lying on the bed.

Finn pressed his ear against Crow's chest and listened to his heart beat. "What do you think our kids will be like?"

Crow's *hmm* vibrated through Finn. "They'll be stubborn and probably too serious. I'll apologize for it in advance because I'm sure they'll get that from me. Maybe they'll get some of your joy for life to counteract it."

Finn smiled and traced his name across Crow's stomach. "I'll teach them the silks, and you can teach them to shoot. We'll even get them their own little Rufus. They can zap people that tug on their tails."

"No one's tugging on my kid's tail or I'm shooting their ass." Crow scowled and stroked a hand down Finn's fluffy tail. "Your tail is included there too."

Fin chuckled. "Okay, big guy. Do you think Dermot and your mom will come visit?"

"Yes." Crow seemed very sure, and Finn hoped he was right. He didn't like the idea of taking Diana's son away from her.

"Will Diana be okay without you? It wasn't too long ago that she was a grieving mess."

Crow kissed the top of Finn's head. "She'll be alright. She has a purpose now. Before Dad died, her life revolved around him and the family. Now, she has a business and a family in her crew."

Finn sighed. "Okay. I'll try not to worry about it. So, Brisco is coming with us so he can follow Death around and irritate him. Why do you think Parker wants to come?"

Crow sniffed. "He *is* my friend."

Finn leaned back and gave Crow a look. "While I'm sure that's part of it, that can't be *all* of it."

Crow snorted. "That's the truth. I don't know. I think Parker is as ready for a change as I am."

Finn's comm chimed, and he reached across Crow and grabbed it. "Halli sent an update."

"How's she doing?"

"Most of the Vextonians are on their way to one of the safe havens. There are still some that have been harder to find, but she's working on tracing them. We're getting there." Finn let his eyes close. "Three months in, and we're making good progress."

Finn rested in Crow's arms and thought about the report he had gotten from Audre about Vextonar. While the fighting was over, most of the planet was abandoned and there was no government left. The Primes that had ruled Vextonar were no more.

Wineon had sold such a large portion of the population, but many had left as soon as they were able so they could search for their loved ones or join up in the fight against Humans First. The ones that stayed either didn't have much choice or were fully supportive of HF.

Now, everyone left was just tired. The city planet was a barren rock, and its people were displaced. *I hope the Vextonians have a home to return to when this is all over.*

His comm chimed again with an incoming call. He saw who it was and grinned. "Dannol."

His friend's happy face projected above his comm. "What are you doing lying in bed, Finn? Is that Aiden?"

Crow cleared his throat. "Hi, Dannol. It's nice to meet you finally."

"Finn's been hiding you away from me." Dannol shook his head, trying to look stern. "Plus, I had to learn about the baby from the Lord Admiral."

Finn sat up. "Wait, Fasi knows? I just found out, damn it. How is it that I'm not even on Charybdis Station and gossip still travels this fast?"

Dannol's image blurred as Finn's friend bounced in his seat. "I spoke to Ms. Diana too. She said you two were settling on the station after the Vextonians are found."

"You spoke with my mom?" Crow sounded amused.

Dannol nodded, grinning. "Then Meggie, Nessa, and I went in and cleaned up your house, Finn. It's such a bachelor's pad. It was kinda embarrassing having to explain your aerial silks to Nessa, and

Meggie *may* have rifled through your underwear drawer."

"Really, Dannol? Really?" Finn narrowed his eyes. "Why do you look guilty?"

"You know everyone already knew about your fancy undies." Dannol's eyes wouldn't meet his. "Selene had to keep telling you to wear more practical underwear when we were in training."

"Dannol?"

"Okay, so Meggie blabbed to a few more folks, and now people keep dropping fancy underwear off at your house. Fire likes them too, so he's been searching through the boxes they leave on your porch."

Finn groaned. "The blue fleet doesn't need to know what their lieutenant wears under his uniform."

Dannol gave him a bright smile. "Well, now they do, and you have some nice new things waiting on you when you get back."

Crow started laughing and that set Dannol to giggling. The Havenite could never resist laughing with someone.

Finn leaned over and bit Crow's shoulder. "Maybe we shouldn't live on the station."

16

SUGARWORM SYSTEM, PLANET RUEAL

*C*row was a little sad to be leaving Degran's ship, and he'd never thought he would think that about a slave ship. Finn and he had spent most of the trip holed up together talking and loving on one another. It had been a nice reprieve.

He looked at the determined people filling Finn's conference room. *The reprieve is officially over.*

Finn's captains, Leslie, and Fasi spread out around the room. Moyra was back from the Weasel's base and looking grim. Roxy sat in her lap and rubbed her head against Moyra's chin to comfort her.

Finn sat in Crow's lap and reviewed his notes on his tablet. "Of the two million seventy-five thousand three hundred and twenty-two missing Vextonians, we've recovered one million five hundred and seventy thousand two hundred and sixteen."

"Dramacus is honoring their word?" Weber asked, expression amazed. "I guess it's a good thing Death is still on their planet."

Fasi looked disgusted. "Verion and Wyatt will stay there until all the Vextonians are away, just in case Xaran tries to renege on the agreement."

Finn sighed. "According to Teresa Malone's ledgers, sixteen thousand three hundred and fifty-two died on the way to Rueal. We've discovered the rest of the Vextonians went to the Weasel. It's been months since they were sent to him."

Moyra stood, keeping Roxy in her arms. "Noe and a few other Full Moon operatives are still in the Weasel's base. We've scoured the place as well as we could and most of the remaining Vextonians are there."

"Most?" Ronnie asked.

"They have several large warehouses that are housing over a million slaves." Moyra stroked a hand down Roxy's back. "Alber hacked their systems, and a large portion of our missing Vextonians are still there."

Weber grinned. "This is good news. He could have sold them all across the galaxy by now."

Moyra smirked. "For some reason, moving them has gotten a little harder lately."

Fasi snorted. "Charbydis Station and our allies are making it hell for anyone trying to keep them."

"Some aren't there though." Finn bit his lip, and Crow felt a surge of sympathy for his mate. "Ezvin isn't there."

Moyra gave him a sad look. "Not according to the records. All they say is that Ezvin and twelve other Vextonians were sold together on the black auction. We can't find who they went to."

"We'll find them," Weber said. Each captain in the room looked just as determined.

Crow hugged Finn and almost laughed when Finn rubbed his head against Crow's chin, just like Roxy was currently doing to Moyra. "What's it going to cost us to take out the pirate base?" he asked.

Moyra eyed him. "Good question. Their defenses are impressive. From what I can tell, no other planet in the system knows they're there. Hell, Aruta doesn't seem to pay attention to any of their moons, and one of their other moons is actually habitable to a range of species."

"Can we get in?" Finn asked.

Moyra shrugged. "If we were just taking them out, we could destroy their atmospheric shield and be done with them. However, we want to keep the slaves alive. My people can disable their long-range weapons from within and we can land. From there, it's going to be a hard fight."

"Can our ships take out any of their buildings from the air before landing?" Crow asked.

Moyra looked conflicted. "I want to say yes, but these people have their own slaves outside of the ones they sell. We'll have a lot of civilian casualties if we do that."

"I wish we had Death with us." Finn sighed. "We can't depend on him for everything though, and if we move him from Dramacus, King Xaran is likely to try something."

Fasi rubbed his furry chin. "What are their numbers like?"

"About even with ours." Moyra nodded at Leslie. "That's counting all of the green fleet that's here on Rueal too."

Ronnie whistled. "That's a lot of pirates."

"He's the worst in the system." Crow scowled. "Occasionally, one of the planets would try to find him and take him out, but no one had any luck."

"Not until now." Fasi grinned and stood. "I'll talk to the rest of the planets in the system and get us more ships. I want to outnumber them when we go in. Let's sabotage them from within and overwhelm them from the outside."

Crow eyed the man. "Aren't you supposed to go straight back to Charybdis Station? Wasn't that what you told Dru?"

"I recall him saying that." Otto gave the Lord Admiral a hard look. "We're supposed to borrow a ship from the green lieutenant and return to the station."

Fasi made a face. "Fuck that. I can help here, and I just so happen to be here. We'll leave when I'm ready."

Otto and everyone else in the room groaned while Crow just smiled. *Fasi Juren really is the strangest planetary leader I know.*

———

LATER THAT NIGHT, CROW, FINN, AND THE OTHERS gathered in Diana's villa again. Crow had started thinking of the place as his mom's home. Dermot and Jenise were already settled into the house Dermot and he had grown up in, and they had made it their own. Diana had quickly made the villa her own too.

"Are you two going to mind if I move to Charybdis Station?" Crow asked. Dermot and he sat in his mom's office while she finished up some paperwork.

Diana looked up and smiled. "I'll miss you, baby boy, but I'm not going to mind. I think it's the best choice for you and Finn."

Dermot yawned and nodded. "Same here. I'll miss seeing you all the time, but you have a new life to make now that Mom's taking your old one over."

Diana rolled her eyes while Dermot and Crow laughed.

Crow hesitated a moment, then smoothed a hand over his abdomen. His jacket was thick and easily covered the very slight bulge. "I'm pregnant."

Diana's tablet clattered to the desk, and Dermot's mouth dropped open.

"Way to give me a damn heart attack, Aiden. You're pregnant already?" Dermot asked.

He smiled. "Mom was the one who reminded me birth control is always a little finicky for hybrids."

Diana sat back in her chair and wiped at her eyes. "Oh, Aiden. This is good news. Gods, I hope your child takes after Finn."

Crow laughed hard enough to snort. "You aren't the only one."

She shook her head. "I'll be visiting Charybdis Station often, son. You and Finn are going to be good parents."

He licked his lips. "How is it you go right to what's worrying me?"

"I know you." She gave him a look. "You're just like me and overthink everything. Being a parent is even scarier than being in love, Aiden. I know you'll figure it out though."

"We'll still be here for you too." Dermot punched his shoulder. "We're just a call away, and Mom won't be the only one taking a vacation." He grinned. "Jenise is going to be so jealous. We just started to try for kids."

Crow smiled wryly. "It was unexpected." He was quiet for a minute. "You'll both help Jada, right?"

Diana nodded. "The election is next week, and we're voting for her. The senate is pissed that she's running because she's a hybrid, but the only way this place will really change is if someone keeps stirring it up."

"Senate elections are next year." Dermot grinned. "A couple of Dad's friends are thinking about putting their names in for consideration to represent Pagent's Distillery."

Crow nodded. Rueal would come back better than before. He felt lighter after talking to them about leaving. He had clung to the planet because its future was important to his dad. Now, he felt like he could finally start to plan his own future.

A knock at the door interrupted them.

Lumi leaned in and grinned at them. "Lunch is ready, and you might want to hurry before it's all gone."

Diana chuckled. "Finn's people sure eat a lot."

"I love it." Lumi danced in place. "It's nice to have a job that I picked myself. I made your favorite, Diana."

She stood and smiled. "Thanks, Lumi. We'll come now."

Crow followed his mom and brother from the office. He looked around until he found Finn. His mate sat curled up next to the window watching the rain. Roxy sprawled across his lap, wings gently flapping in her sleep.

Sandve, Amelia, and Weber sat with him, talking quietly. Finn smiled softly at something one of them said, and Crow's heart sped up.

"You're worse than a teenager." Diana shook her head. "Look at those eyes, Dermot."

"They're basically hearts. It's ridiculous."

Crow shoved his brother. "You were worse when you met Jenise."

Dermot laughed. "Yeah, probably."

Fasi, in shifted form, came in and shook the rain from his body.

Lumi tsked. "We have a mudroom in the back, Lord Admiral, and I know I told you about it before you went for a run."

Fasi looked up and gave the former slave a pitiful look.

Lumi's stern expression disappeared. "Oh, you're too cute to scold."

Moyra snorted. "You get use to him after a while, Lumi. Then you can scold to your heart's content."

Fasi ignored them and headed toward the back of the house. A few minutes later, he came back in, shifted and dressed. "I do miss going for runs. I never seem to have the time back home."

Crow went to sit next to Finn while Lumi started loading down the table with food. "You look sleepy."

Finn nodded, eyes heavy. "I am. I think your pregnancy is wearing me out."

Amelia snorted. "That's not how it works, Finn."

Sandve leaned closer to Crow. "The Lord Admiral contacted the political leaders of Aruta, Rueal, and Tammol. They're sending ships to help with the attack on the pirate base."

"We're calling it Operation Weasel." Finn snickered. "Seriously, why would he choose that name?"

Crow shook his head. "We'll need to talk to him. Is anyone in charge of locating and restraining him during the attack?"

"Moyra has Noe on it," Sandve said.

Finn held his arms out. "Enough work talk. Snuggle me, then let's go eat. The damn pregnancy has me starving."

Crow gently slid Finn and Roxy into his lap. "My pleasure."

17

SUGARWORM SYSTEM, ESINDA -
SMALLEST MOON OF PLANET ARUTA

inn stood behind the captain's chair on the bridge of the Blue Albatross. His ship was one of his fleet's heavy hitters and carried a large number of soldiers. Crow and Fasi stood with him while Weber directed the pilots, and Rufus circled above them all.

"Alber is worth more than we pay him." Fasi shook his head as they watched a door to the space port open, over and over again. The pirates clearly thought it was a glitch in their systems and not shuttles carrying soldiers into the base.

"That's the truth." Finn bit his lip as another large shuttle signaled they had entered the spaceport. "It will take a while to get everyone in, but with our shields, this just may work."

Charybdis Station shuttles and smaller grade ships were transporting their soldiers into the base while their allies gathered on the other side of the moon. With luck, they would be well prepared for the ground attack before the Weasel or his people even knew they were there.

Finn turned to Crow. "You'll stay on the ship with Fasi, right?"

Crow snorted. "No. We had this conversation already, Finn."

"I think we should have it again until you agree to stay on the ship with Fasi."

Crow tugged him into his arms and gave him a soft kiss. "I'll watch my back, but I'm watching yours too. I'll pick a high spot on one of the warehouses and keep an eye on you. Deal with it."

Weber stood. "Time to load up in the shuttle, everyone who is going. Ignali, keep us in contact with everyone."

"Yes, sir." Ignali tipped his chin up. "Lieutenant, where did the Lord Admiral go?"

Finn looked around. "He was just here. Sandve?"

The operative looked around, groaning. "I was watching the shuttles. Damn it. I'll check the restrooms."

"I'll check his quarters." Otto shook his head. "The man is too big to lose this easily."

"Good job there, operatives." Brisco chuckled. "I'd mock you more, but the Lord Admiral is tricky. Good luck."

Finn wished he could say goodbye to Fasi, but he couldn't wait. "Let's go." He took Crow's hand, and they hurried to the shuttle. "You have extra shields?"

"Yes. Do you?"

Finn grinned. "Yes. Be careful."

"You too, love." Crow leaned over and kissed him. "Brisco is staying on your ass, and Parker is with me."

Brisco whooped. "Let's go pirate hunting!"

Parker shook his head. "He makes me feel old."

"You are old," Brisco said over his shoulder.

"You're two years older than me." Parker scowled and shoved Brisco.

They loaded into the shuttle, and in less than an hour, they were inside the pirate base.

Finn watched out the window as they silently flew above the heads of the Weasel's engineers gathered around the docking controls. "You know, ever since we got a hold of Full Moon's tech, our battles have gotten a lot easier. Can you imagine trying to take this place without it?"

"No." Crow sighed. "This guy has been a problem in the system for a while. I wish we could have found the base and gotten rid of him sooner."

The shuttle landed in an empty corner, and they quickly unloaded so the shuttle could leave before someone ran into it.

Finn held tightly to Crow's hand as long as he could, but they reached the entrance to the spaceport too quickly. "Be careful," he whispered one more time before heading to his assigned position with Brisco.

Finn and Brisco were joining the soldiers taking one of the three barracks. Finn grabbed a spot near a window and waited.

"I hate waiting," Brisco whispered. "It's worse than being disemboweled."

"Have you ever been disemboweled?" Finn asked, amused.

"Well, no, but this is definitely worse."

Finn rolled his eyes and watched the men and women inside the barracks. *At least it doesn't look like there are any slaves inside.*

Clearly someone came to clean up after the messy bastards, but Finn couldn't see anyone in there at the moment.

"Go time." Ignali's voice came through the line. "Follow your orders exactly."

Finn heard the noise in the spaceport from where he stood. Their allies were charging it. Moyra's people had disabled the pulse cannons and long-range weapons, which meant their allies were able to shoot their way in without too many casualties. Hopefully.

Brisco broke the glass in the window they stood next to, and Finn tossed one of Beck's pulse grenades into the large front room. The electric shocks shot through the room, frying each of the pirates within.

Finn could hear glass breaking and more screams from the rest of the barracks. *First attack is a success.*

Pirates began flooding the room as they came from farther inside the barracks.

Brisco and Finn took turns throwing grenades inside until the pirates began firing toward their position. Finn directed Rufus into the room, and his bot began shooting a path through the pirates firing at them.

"Let's switch windows." Brisco tugged Finn to another window, and they repeated their tactic.

Eventually, pirates stopped coming through the room. They were either all dead or had found another exit.

"Clearing out barrack three now." One of his soldiers' voices came through the comm in Finn's ear.

"Heading to barrack two." Finn tugged Brisco, and they ran toward the next of the huge buildings. They were supposed to check to make sure all barracks were taken care of before moving on to the warehouses.

Barrack two was in the same state as the previous one, but pirates had overwhelmed the Charybdis Station soldiers in barrack one. The fighting was already intense as more pirates joined the fight from a nearby bar.

"Fuck. Fighting is dirty at barrack one," Finn said into his comm, then engaged his shield's visibility so no one would accidently shoot him."

He launched into the fight using his altered gravity boots and landed on top of one of the pirates, his blade already slicing into the back of the man's neck.

Rufus buzzed around him, taking every shot that Finn directed. Finn spun and kicked a charging pirate, then stabbed into his chest before knocking the man down and hopping over him, pulling his blade free as he moved.

The fighting went fast, and Finn focused on taking out the people closest to him. He didn't notice the man running toward him from behind until he was almost upon him.

Finn spun and blocked the man's blade but felt a burning pain in his side. He cried out, and his arm lost its strength. The pirate's blade pressed closer to him as he fell to his knees.

His arm finally gave way, and the man's grinning face filled Finn's view. Then the man was gone, tackled by a large purple Grell in shifted form. The Lord Admiral tore the screaming man's throat out, then came to stand over Finn, growling at any that approached.

"Damn it, Fasi. Hack will kill me if you die." Finn tried to focus on directing Rufus to take out the pirates approaching, but he could barely keep his eyes open.

Shots came from above, and the pirates started falling fast. *My mate really is a good shot.* Pain was spreading fast, and Finn's vision dimmed.

———

WHEN HE WOKE AGAIN, HE WAS IN THE MED BAY OF THE Blue Albatross. The beds were full of wounded soldiers, and doctors and nurses rushed around.

"Finn?" Crow's voice was thick with tears.

Finn moved his head, wincing at the pain. "Aiden. I'm sorry. I got hurt."

Crow was a disheveled mess, his eyes bloodshot. "I saw it all. You scared the shit out of me."

"Is Fasi okay?"

Crow's laugh was rough. "He's fine. He had a few cuts and bruises, but he saved your ass."

"So did you." Finn smiled, already feeling his eyes closing again. "You had our backs."

"Not quick enough."

Finn tried to tell him to stop being dramatic, but he was asleep again before the words could get out.

The next time he awoke, the med bay was a little calmer. Crow still sat beside him, his facial hair a testament to how long Finn had been unconscious. *Two, maybe three days.*

Amelia slept in another chair near his bed. She looked as tired as Finn felt.

"Thirsty," Finn managed to say.

Crow startled and grabbed his hand.

Amelia woke up at the sound of his voice and sat up fast. "Oh sweetheart. You're awake." She hurried to get him a glass of water and held it for Finn to sip from. "The doctor needs to come look you over again."

"The mission?"

"We took the base." Crow waved his hand to one of the nurses passing by. "He's awake again."

"Casualties?"

Crow gave him a sad look. "It was rough. The pirates fought hard. Our allies lost close to a hundred all together, and between your and Leslie's fleets, we lost forty-six."

Finn squeezed his eyes shut. "Damn it. My captains? Brisco and Parker?"

"They all made it." Crow laughed roughly. "Brisco is pissed he wasn't there to save you."

"Fasi is in big trouble."

"No, he isn't." Crow shook his head. "He's my fucking hero. The asshole snuck down with us and helped out where he could."

"I'm still gonna yell at him." Finn winced as he tried to lift his hand. "Are my ears and tail still there?"

Amelia laughed. "That's what you're worried about? Yes, your ears and tail are fine. Your innards aren't so good. You were shot in the gut, sweetheart. You almost died."

"I'm sorry." Finn sniffed. "I didn't mean to scare you all."

Crow squeezed his fingers and swallowed hard. "I can't lose you, Finn."

"I see you're finally awake." Fasi, Otto, and Sandve walked toward Finn's bed. "You're still too pale, son."

"You're in big trouble." Finn tried to glare, but it hurt. "Are you sure my ears are okay?" he asked Crow.

Crow rolled his eyes. "Your ears are still adorable, love. I promise."

"I don't feel my tail."

Crow waved Finn's tail at him. "See, it really is okay. You're just so out of it on pain meds. You shouldn't feel anything for a while."

Fasi sat next to him and took his other hand. "You scared us, Finn. Hack had to do some talking to keep Dannol from stealing a ship and flying here to get you."

Otto smiled down at him. "Despite the losses, the mission was a success. The Vextonians were recovered, along with a whole hell of a lot of other slaves."

"The thirteen missing?" Finn asked. "Ezvin?"

Crow shook his head. "No Ezvin."

"The Weasel is in a cell." Fasi looked grim. "Noe and Moyra are interrogating him now."

Finn tried to sit up. "I want to see."

Crow cursed. "Damn it, Finn. Stay there. What part of *you almost died* did you not understand? You're lucky to be conscious right now."

Finn came close to whining. "I want to see Moyra and Noe beat up the Weasel."

"Finn, you need to rest," Amelia said.

"Please?" Finn asked, voice plaintive.

"Gods damn it." Fasi pulled up his tablet, scowling as he did something on it. "Here. You can watch it."

Finn sniffled, then smiled. "Thanks."

On the screen of Fasi's tablet, Moyra and Noe sat across a table from a Human-Drall hybrid. The man was big, and he looked like he'd already been worked over.

The Weasel practically pouted. "I don't know where they are. We sell slaves all around the galaxy. I can't possibly keep track of them all. The only reason my warehouses were full is because of you fuckers and your damn threats against those who bought the Vextonians. They're just property. It was no big deal until your stupid station made it one."

Noe flipped a throwing knife over and over in his hand. "Can I kill him?"

"No." Moyra sounded sad. "I think we're supposed to be the good guys or something like that."

The Weasel smirked. "Sorry, I can't help you."

Noe's blade flew across the table and pinned the Weasel's hand to the table. The man screamed in pain.

"Noe, good guys, remember?" Moyra didn't seem too horribly upset.

Another blade flew through the air and pinned the

Weasel's other hand to the chair arm. Noe pulled a third knife from his vest. "He's not dead."

"I suggest you tell us where they are before he tries to pin your dick to the chair." Moyra grinned and batted her eyes. "Actually, can you wait until after? I want to see if his aim is that good. I mean, there's a table over your lap."

Noe slid from his chair. "Look, Moyra. It's that easy. I can see his crouch from here. No problem."

"I can't tell you." Sweat covered the Weasel's face, and he was pale from pain. "They'll kill me."

Moyra snorted. "We'll kill you if you don't, and I can guarantee to make it as painful as possible. My buddy Alber can fiddle with the recordings to make it look like you tried to escape. Then, it's all *'Oops! Sorry, Lord Admiral. I slipped and my blade stabbed him twenty-eight times. No, sir, I don't know how his dick got cut off.'*"

"I didn't think he could get paler," Finn whispered, eyes wide.

"Why is Moyra always threatening to cut a dick off?" Sandve asked. "She could be a little more creative. What about boiling or being eaten alive by rodents?"

"Okay," the Weasel said, voice thick with pain.

Otto gave Sandve a look. "Clearly her methods work just fine."

"Fuck, okay." The Weasel looked close to passing out. "Get these things out of my hands."

"After you talk." Noe kept his face bland. "Where are they?"

"There's this resort. It's real selective and private. The only people who know about it are members and those that work there. I work for them a lot. When a certain type of slave crosses my path, I send them there."

"What type?" Moyra asked, voice quiet.

"Young and pretty." The man kept his eyes on the table. "They like to get them young so they can start training and conditioning them. Omiri is my contact there." His eyes darted up when Moyra started pacing as she eyed him in disgust. "Don't look at me like that. They don't fuck them right away or anything. I'm not a monster. They just put them on a special diet and start cosmetic surgery to fix any flaws. Omiri likes to make sure they're nice and subservient before training them as bed slaves when they turn twelve."

Finn growled, ears flat. "Kill him. Kill the fucking monster."

Fasi squeezed his hand. "After he tells us where."

Moyra stilled. "Where is the resort, and who are the members?"

"It's on Fire Veil in the Silverlight System. All the leaders of Humans First were members, but some of the other planetary leaders were too. You've killed most of them, so I don't know who all is there now." The Weasel started swaying. "Can I see a doctor now?"

Another blade flew through the air and landed in the center of the man's forehead. The Weasel went lax in his chair, dead.

"Damn it, Noe. I wanted to make it hurt more." Moyra glared at the other operative.

"It slipped," Noe said, voice dry.

Fasi turned off the tablet. "We know where to go. We'll find him, Finn."

Otto squeezed Fasi's shoulder. "You're going back to the station, Lord Admiral. Crow and Finn can handle this. It's a long trip to the Silverlight System. Finn can heal up so he's in peak condition to kick some ass."

Fasi growled. "I don't want to go."

Finn closed his eyes, feeling sleep creeping up. He was so tired, and he kept seeing Ezvin and Hazel's smiling faces. "Remember to take Amelia home too."

"Maybe I don't want to go either," Amelia said and pressed a hand to his forehead. "My sweet boy, you need to rest."

"Finn and me will find them, Fasi. You and Amelia can go home now." Crow's deep voice soothed Finn, and he let himself go.

They *would* find Ezvin and make the people who hurt him pay.

18

SILVERLIGHT SYSTEM, EN ROUTE TO
PLANET FIRE VEIL

*C*row dozed in one of the large chairs in their quarters aboard the Blue Albatross. Finn sat curled in his lap, fiddling with his medallion while he spoke with Halli on his tablet.

"Tammol said they could take in more if we need them to, but considering they took in all of those we found on Dramacus, I'm worried we'll strain them too much. I'll talk to Audre when we're finished on Fire Veil and see when we can start sending the Vextonians back home. I think she wants to make sure the new government and economic trade routes are in place so they don't all starve to death if we leave them there."

"The first wave of Vextonians are settled in their temporary homes. The second wave are in transport, but most are near their destinations. The latest wave just began their journey." Halli looked better rested than normal. The Fallon's skin was brighter, and the bags under her eyes were starting to fade. "The last of the Vextonians are being secured. It'll take a little time to process them and send them to safety, but we're getting there, Finn."

A feather tickled Crow's nose. Roxy sat behind him on the back of the chair. She had grown over the last month, so she didn't quite fit. She compensated by bracing her front half on Crow's shoulder and had one wing spread over his head.

This is my life now. I'm a chair for my mate and his hiss beast. Finn stroked a hand over Crow's slight baby bump. *And a house for our baby.* A year ago, Crow would never have thought he'd be so content and at peace with this life.

"We should reach Fire Veil in a couple of days." Finn rubbed his eyes and yawned. "After we rescue Ezvin and the others, it's just a matter of getting people to the right place."

Halli looked concerned. "Are you healthy enough to do this? Weber told me he and the other captains could handle things."

Finn rolled his eyes. "I'm perfectly well."

Crow snorted. "He is not perfectly well. It's been less than a month. His innards are still recovering, though he's mobile now and not at risk of dying from his injuries. The doctor said he needed to rest and take it easy."

Finn's ears flattened, and he glared at Crow. "I can handle this."

"Oh, I know you can." Crow placed a kiss on one black fuzzy ear. "You're one of the strongest people I know. I'm just saying you aren't *perfectly well*."

Halli chuckled. "I'll leave you two to argue. I'll see you at the meeting in the morning."

Finn set his tablet aside and watched Crow for a moment. "You've been worried about something lately."

Crow smiled wryly. "How the hell do you notice stuff like that? You're constantly working or resting, and we've only really known each other for a short time." *Also, I thought I hid my nerves better than I obviously have.*

"You're my mate." Finn leaned up and gave him a gentle kiss. "I'll always do my best to notice you no matter how busy or tired I am. I can't promise I'll be perfect, but I'll try my hardest. Now, what's wrong?"

"I thought I lost you, Finn." Crow let out a deep breath, shoulders losing some of their tension. He hadn't realized he'd been carrying it around for as long as he had. "I'm scared I'll lose you. Maybe it'll be in this next fight. Maybe you'll get sick. Hell, maybe you'll end up seeing me the way I see myself and leave me. Losing Dad was hard, and life became almost meaningless. All I could think of was getting back at Jevio, Malone, and HF. It's hard to live again. I don't know what I'd do if I lost you too."

Finn leaned his head against Crow's chest. "I want to tell you that I'll never leave you, but there are things I can't control. I can promise that I'll never willingly leave you. You're a good man, Aiden. One day, you're going to realize it, and I'll be right there by your side."

Crow spit out a feather from Roxy's wing. "You swear?"

Finn looked up, golden eyes luminous. "I swear it. I want to see where you and I go from here. I want to see our baby born. If it's a girl, I want to name her Hazel. If it's a boy, I want to name him Perick. I don't want to forget the pain of losing our loved ones, but I want to move on and be happy with you."

Crow closed his eyes and felt the last of his uncertainty slip away. "Then that's what we'll do. Here on out, I'm all in, Finn. You're mine and I'm yours."

Roxy settled her head next to his and started purring.

Finn smiled, eyes shining. "Roxy is yours too."

Crow sighed. "Yeah. The fucking hiss beast is mine too."

Finn's tablet chimed with an incoming call and he yawned. "Everyone wants to talk today." He answered the call. "Oh, hey Juniper."

Crow hadn't met this friend yet. The Fallon looked a little harried. That didn't stop him from smiling at Finn and Crow.

"You must be Crow." Juniper blew a strand of his golden hair from his eyes. "I've been meaning to give you a call and say hello."

"Finn tells me you're a busy man." Crow sighed when Roxy leaned further onto his shoulder so she could see Juniper.

"That's no excuse." Juniper made a face. "The diner is much more manageable now that Tempest and her mom are helping me. We just hired a new cook too and she's wonderful."

Finn gave the screen a curious look. "Why do you

look so out of sorts then?"

Juniper gave them a guilty look. "So, we wanted to do something special for you two since Crow is leaving his home to be with you."

"Uh oh." Finn groaned. "What happened?"

"Well, first Mo and Pops decided you needed some Druffle."

"Of course they did." Finn looked resigned. "How many did I end up with?"

Juniper smiled apologetically. "Not as many as Draif. Yet. They started installing tunnels and Pops got it in his head that your house was too small since Crow is pregnant."

"For the love of catnip, it has three bedrooms. What did he do?" Finn asked, eyes wide.

"He's adding a second floor and remodeling the first floor to be more spacious." Juniper winced. "Dannol and I packed your things. We'll move everything back in when we're done."

"I really love Pops, even if he can be a bit much." Finn's eyes were soft. "I guess that's not too bad."

"That's not all." Juniper wrinkled his nose. "I thought I would do some landscaping to go with your renovations so I planted a Rueal sundrop rose bush to make Crow feel more at home."

"Thanks?" Finn said, eyeing his friend. "Why do I get the feeling that didn't turn out like you wanted?"

Juniper winced. "Sebastian has a new apprentice, and she decided to *help* the rose bush. Now, your whole yard and half of Dannol's is full of them. I'm transplanting them all over the neighborhood."

Crow chuckled. "Why do I get the feeling things like this are normal for Charybdis Station?"

———

Silverlight System, Planet Fire Veil

Two days later, their fleet arrived at Fire Veil. From space, the red planet looked like it was on fire. It was small, much smaller than Vextonar and Union Station. Crow knew the atmosphere was breathable, but the heat was almost unbearable. A small spaceport was located in the northern hemisphere, but it had to use an artificial atmosphere to maintain a livable temperature.

Finn stood on the bridge with Weber, each of his other captains pulled up on vid-screens. Crow sat with Brisco and Parker. He held Roxy in his lap and watched his mate carefully. Finn had started working out on his silks to build up his strength, and Crow was afraid he'd pushed himself too hard.

"Noe is on the planet now." Moyra made a face. "He says the place is a piece of shit, but we knew that. It's not a fuel stop. It's just meant as a base for hunters and prospectors."

"The Weasel didn't say where the resort was, but surely it has to be obvious." Althea made a face. "The wealthy elite wouldn't want to go through Fire Veil's spaceport. It would be too obvious for one thing, but it really is a piece of shit."

"Moyra, can Alber hack into the spaceport's

defenses?" Crow asked. "If it is involved with this resort, we'll see some sign of it in the tech they use. They should be as junky as the docks and base."

Moyra looked thoughtful. "If they're not, then we know they have more money and connections than expected. Good idea. I'll get him to do it."

"We're scanning the surface of the planet as well." Weber tilted his head toward Ignali. "Likely, it's as well shielded as the pirate base was."

"Okay. Report back in one hour. We'll see what we've discovered." Finn disconnected from his captains and went to stand beside Berenna.

She stood at the viewport, watching the planet approach. "He's down there."

Crow set Roxy on Parker's lap and went to stand on her other side. "We'll get him back."

Finn wrapped an arm around her waist. "Then, the two of you will meet Ival on Vextonar. Will you stay there or go to live on Genarg?"

"Genarg." Berenna seemed certain. "I'm done with Vextonar. I know some of the others want to go back and make it a better home, but I just want to get away from it and all the memories it holds. Life was never easy there."

"Plus, you have two Crellic babies to take care of," Finn reminded her with a smile. "Genarg is their birth home."

They stood together and did their best to distract Berenna from her worries. An hour passed quickly.

Moyra grinned. "Alber didn't have to go far into their systems. They have tech resembling that of both the pirates and the Belcrest assassins. What do you want to bet the resort is nearby, and the spaceport is a front?"

"The Belcrest guild keeps popping up." Weber scowled. "Where are they based again?"

Moyra gave them a blank look. "Uh, Union Station and Vextonar, I think."

Finn groaned. "Do you think they would be involved in the security here?"

"They're assassins, not mercs." Brisco looked thoughtful. "Why would they be here?"

"If their base of operations is in flux, then they may be taking any job they can," Moyra said, shrugging. "That's all speculation though. I'll have Noe do some digging. Hold tight for a little while longer."

Two hours later, Noe had politely *questioned* one of the spaceport managers. The resort was twenty miles north of the spaceport, in a mountain range off limits to hunters. It was also heavily guarded and shielded with more than an atmospheric shield.

"Fuck." Crow stood with Finn and watched the images from the scan. The resort looked impenetrable. "Nothing is ever easy."

Moyra rolled her shoulders. "Okay. Full Moon goes in and sabotages the defenses?"

"Can you get over the walls and through the shields?" Finn asked, eyes narrowed in thought.

Moyra looked over her shoulder, then back at them. "Alber says he could if given time, but it will take a while. They're better than the pirate base."

"The Weasel sends slaves here, right? What if he

sent a few more?" Finn rubbed his chin and his tail swayed in the air behind him. "At the very least, they would open the front door to inspect them."

Moyra started to grin. "My operatives could sneak in while the guards were distracted."

"Bring down the shield and I can lead the fleet in, taking out the towers and pulse cannons," Weber said.

"Have Noe ask the spaceport manager the normal process the Weasel goes through. I imagine he doesn't usually come himself." Finn smiled widely. "I'll go take a shower. I'll need to look my best."

"Whoa." Crow held his hands up. "You're still recovering, and we don't even know if the Weasel brings older slaves."

Finn's brow furrowed. "Did you just call me old?"

Crow rolled his eyes when the other captains laughed at them. "No, fluffball. You'd be a wonderful addition to their resort."

"So would I." Berenna turned away from the window, face determined. "I'll go with Finn too."

Crow smiled sadly. "Berenna, you're pregnant. While you are absolutely beautiful, I can almost guarantee they don't want a pregnant slave at this kind of resort."

"That goes for you too," she said, arching a brow.

Crow huffed. "I'll be going as a guard or something."

Finn cleared his throat. "Do I have any say in this?"

Crow gave him a hard look. "Do I have any say in *you* going down there?"

Finn sighed. "No."

19

THE CREVICE RESORT ON PLANET
FIRE VEIL

F inn ran a hand over the gauzy white fabric of his tight vest as he waited with the others. It covered the scars from his recent injuries and went well with the white lace and satin underwear and garter belt he wore. The only things he didn't like about his outfit were the uncomfortable white slippers he wore and the temporary slave tattoo on his hand.

Rufus was shielded and floating above his head, out of sight but not out of mind. The bot was Finn's only weapon.

Noe had explained that more than just the Weasel dropped off a variety of slaves at the resort. According to Noe's new friend, the slavers brought their selections straight to the resort's back door and let Omiri look them over to see if she was interested.

Typically, a few guards and the slaves took a shuttle to the resort, so Finn and the others had kept their party simple.

While there had looked to be hundreds of guards

around the perimeter, their shuttle was waved through the entrance with only a few questions asked.

A few moments later, they stood at the back door. Finn, Brisco, and several Charybdis Station soldiers were dressed to impress, and Crow and Parker played the well-armed guards.

"This place sure is fancy." Parker whistled. The resort was a massive structure of red stone that blended in with the mountains around it. From behind, the resort appeared to be surprisingly plain, but from the front, it was a breathtaking combination of stone and glass.

With the atmospheric shield, the temperature was comfortable, even though they could see heat rising from the rocks outside of the resort grounds.

Brisco tugged at his sparkly gold boy shorts. "This isn't where I thought I'd be at thirty-eight."

One of shielded operatives chuckled, and Finn recognized Noe's voice. "We'll make this fast."

An invisible hand settled on his back. He hadn't managed to talk Berenna out of coming. "Thank you for this, Finn," she said quietly.

"Any excuse to wear my favorite lingerie." Finn smoothed his hand over his lace-covered ass.

Crow groaned, and Parker fought back a laugh. Before the conversation could continue, the door opened.

The woman in front of them was a stunningly beautiful human with olive skin and dark, wavy hair. Her robes were red and gold Fallon silk, and a long strand of Fire Veil opals hung around her neck.

The guard behind her was a wall of muscle.

The woman stepped outside and looked all the *slaves* up and down before turning to Crow and Parker. "I haven't seen you before."

"I assume you're Omiri?" Crow asked, smiling.

Damn, even his fake smiles are charming. Finn fought the urge to wrap himself around Crow.

The woman nodded. "Yes. The resort will take these three." She pointed to Finn and two of the other soldiers. She licked her lips as she eyed Brisco and ran a pointed, blood red nail down his chest. "This one, I'll buy for my personal collection. I like mature specimens myself."

Finn held back a laugh at Brisco's flat expression.

"The others I don't want." She waved them away. "The resort will send credits to your account. I trust you left your information at the spaceport?"

"Yes, ma'am." Crow nodded politely. "Thank you for your time."

The guard grunted and waved Finn, Brisco, Olivia, and Marni inside the door. Finn could practically feel the tension coming from Crow. *Trust me, big guy.*

Crow and Parker slowly ushered the other soldiers away and back toward the shuttle. They disappeared from sight as Finn and the others were herded away from the door and into a room full of servants and slaves.

Berenna's hand on his back was a reassuring weight.

"Take them to the slave quarters. Marlanna will deal with them." Omiri pulled Brisco's arm. "You'll come with me. I have the perfect outfit for you, and my assistant can get you acclimated. We're going to have so much fun before I add you to my collection."

Brisco shot him a panicked look, but Finn didn't know what to do. It would take some time for the Full Moon operatives to get in place. *That shit sounds ominous.*

"Berenna," he whispered, confident he wouldn't be heard over the talking around them. "Will you follow Brisco?"

She patted his back, then her hand fell away.

Finn and the others were led through wide halls full of bustling people. Occasionally, he would get a glimpse into one of the front rooms – rooms that were full of opulent furniture and artwork. Clearly, those were the rooms where the resort members spent their time.

Eventually, they entered a small, narrow chamber filled with cots. The guard grunted. "Stay here." He shut and locked the door behind him.

Olivia, a Drall-Wello hybrid, looked around the room. "Not much here. Nothing that would make a weapon."

Marnie, a Fallon-Havenite hybrid, scratched his bearded chin. "This is weird."

"Seriously." Finn went to the door and pressed his ear to it. "I suppose we're supposed to wait for this Marlanna, but I don't like it. Let's shield up and get out of here."

"I can open the door." Olivia came to stand beside

him and worked on the door console. A few moments later, it opened.

"Activate your shields and search for Ezvin and the others. Arm yourselves if you can. If the attack doesn't happen soon, meet back at the backdoor." Finn pressed the small shield pinned to the inside of his garter belt. "I'm going to check on Brisco."

"Yes, sir." Marnie's voice was already moving out the door.

"He hates small spaces," Olivia whispered, then left.

Finn traced their path back down the hall, then turned down the corridor Brisco had been taken. Traffic in the halls grew steadily lighter as he went, trying to peek into each room along the way. The lighting and décor increased in quality, leading Finn to think he was moving into one of the guest areas until the hallway ended at a large, ornate door.

Finn shrugged and pressed the console. The door cracked, and he looked in.

Omiri lay on the floor, the hole in her head likely from the phaser Berenna held. Three large guards also lay dead around the room. One near the door and one next to Omiri. The third lay next to the surgical table Brisco was strapped to.

Berenna stood over a kneeling slave, phaser pressed to the Wello-Dedril hybrid's head.

Finn opened the door the rest of the way and slipped inside, shutting and locking the door behind him. "Berenna? What happened?"

Berenna startled and looked up. She was pale and shaking, but her hand gripped the phaser tightly.

"Brisco's unconscious. Omiri injected him with something, and the guards strapped him to the table. She was going to do something horrible, Finn. Look." She pointed toward the shelving along three of the walls.

"Fuck." Finn swallowed bile. Containers lined each shelf. They were filled with fluid and body parts. There were perfectly preserved heads on one shelf and what looked like hearts on another. Other rows contained different body parts. Things Finn didn't want to dwell too much on. "What the hell is this place?"

"The Mistress's collection room," the kneeling slave said.

Finn narrowed his eyes and watched the slave closely. The woman looked completely unconcerned, and she had a phaser to her head.

"Berenna, why are you holding a phaser on her? She's a slave."

Berenna shook her head. "She's Omiri's assistant. She was helping her. She dressed Brisco in that black outfit he's wearing."

"Did she have a choice?" Finn asked, watching the slave carefully.

The woman didn't seem frightened or worried. She also didn't rush to defend herself. "I serve the Mistress."

"The Mistress is dead." Finn walked over and kicked Omiri. "There is no one to serve anymore."

"I serve the Mistress," the woman repeated.

"Shit." Finn looked around and easily found bindings. *It's a torture chamber. Of course, there are bindings.*

He quickly bound the slave and moved her away from the table.

Berenna wiped at her eyes. "I killed the guards, then the woman. It was easy because I was shielded. They didn't even expect it."

"Nice shots."

"Ival made me learn." She swallowed. "There's something wrong with the slave woman. Omiri was obviously twisted, but that slave isn't all there. What have they done to my baby, Finn?"

Finn shook his head and checked Brisco's vitals. "I don't know, Berenna, but we're getting Ezvin and the others out of here. It looks like Brisco is alive, just unconscious. I'm going to activate our shields and carry him out of here."

"You can't." Berenna shook her head. "Your injuries are still too fresh. I'll stay here with him. Go find my son."

"Shit." Finn rubbed his ears. "Lock the door behind me."

"Okay."

Finn took one of the guard's phaser and vibroblade. "I'll be back as soon as I can."

A loud alert sounded through the wall comms in the room.

"The attack has started. I'll send someone here."

"Thank you." Berenna gripped his shoulder. "I'll protect him. I swear."

Finn left the room and waited until he heard the lock engage before running down the hall. Soldiers wearing the Belcrest insignia filled the halls while the servants and slaves knelt against the walls.

Finn frowned and focused on Rufus. The bot soared in front of him, firing shots, one after another while Finn used the vibroblade to cut down the bewildered guards. By the time he made it to the end of the hallway, more than twenty Belcrest assassins were dead, and his shield was shattered.

He looked back at the slaves and servants. "Stay here, out of the way. We aren't here to harm you."

They just stared, no one willing to speak up. He thought of Donna and Bertie. The two slaves had been willing to help from the start, and they had seen horrible things. *These people have seen some very, very bad shit.*

"Do any of you know where they keep the children?" he asked.

They simply stared at him.

"Okay. I'll find them. Don't worry." Finn shook his head and moved slowly to the next room. Without his shield, he was an obvious target.

The resort shook, and he heard the engine of a ship flying above. Finn grinned and jumped on the next guard he came across, cutting him down quickly while Rufus took out another.

A few more dead guards later, Finn found Marnie with a large group of children, ranging from two years old to twelve. "Where's Olivia?"

Marnie urged the children to hurry. "She's holding off the guards behind me. What's ahead?"

"Just dead guards until you get to the backdoor of the resort. I'll go help Olivia."

"Thanks. I'll get the kids out."

A familiar face caught Finn's attention, and he almost cried. "Ezvin!"

The four-year-old looked up at him, eyes curious.

Finn shook his head and smiled. "It's good to see you, kid. Marnie, take care of them."

"Yes, sir."

Finn pushed past them and ran toward the sound of fighting. Olivia had a phaser, but her shield barely shimmered around her, and she clutched at a wound on her arm from a blade.

Her bot cut through the guards coming through the entrance to the slave quarters, but there were too many.

Finn sent Rufus in to help thin down the guards and ducked behind a cabinet lining the walls. "Olivia, we need to get out of here."

She shook her head and ducked down beside him. "They get past and they'll get the children."

"I could really use a grenade right now." Finn groaned and pulled the phaser from his garter belt. "You know Selene once told me you can't do battle in your underwear?"

Olivia snorted. "Obviously, she was wrong."

Finn fired another shot, then ducked down again. "We're stuck, aren't we?"

"Yes, we are." Olivia's gave him a grim look. "You need to leave. I'll cover you."

"Not happening." Finn fired more shots, then

ducked down again.

"Lieutenant, you have to."

"Fuck that." Finn growled. "I don't leave people behind."

"Neither do we." Moyra's voice came from behind him. "Damn, your ass looks good in that lingerie, Lieutenant."

A shield was pressed into his hand, and he grinned. "You're my favorite captain, Moyra."

"I'm telling Web you said that."

A concussion grenade flew through the air, and Olivia and Finn ducked down low, covering their ears. The line of Belcrest guards thinned considerably.

Finn whooped and activated his shield before running toward the soldiers, blade drawn. With a fresh shield and Olivia and Moyra at his back, they took out the guards quickly. Finn made a note to tell Hack he really needed to promote Olivia.

"Head back to the backdoor or move forward?" Moyra asked.

"Olivia needs a medic," Finn started to say, then he heard a very familiar voice.

"No one is supposed to know about the Crevice. We're supposed to be safe here, yet fucking Charybdis Station is attacking us. I recognize their ship insignias. I demand you get me out of here."

"President Wineon." He laughed. "Oh, we finally found the most hated person in the Silverlight System."

Moyra grinned. "Push forward?"

"Olivia, go join Marnie and the children," Finn ordered.

She snorted. "I'll quote you here, Lieutenant: *fuck that*."

Finn sighed. "I should have known."

They slipped out of the broken door of the slave quarters and down a short hallway. An elaborate archway led to a formal dining room.

Finn crouched low and started counting guards.

Several finely dressed people huddled together across the room while servants and slaves were forced to stand in front of them, making a living wall of protection. *Fuckers.*

The only other door was shut and locked. Finn could hear fighting on the other side of it.

President Wineon stood next to a middle-aged human man. She looked as neatly and modestly dressed as when she last appeared in the media. "You are supposed to guarantee safety and confidentiality, Newland. I should have known better than to trust a bourgeoise family. Your father was a gambler for fuck's sake."

The man's face grew red. "I've given you and everyone else here a place to play your twisted games, Wineon. You and yours aren't any better than me, so don't you dare talk down to me."

Finn shook his head and aimed his phaser at the closest guard. He fired into the woman's shield until it broke. There were sixteen guards in total, and Moyra, Olivia, and Finn took them out quickly. *Thank you, catnip gods, for the Full Moon division's technology.*

Newland shoved Wineon in front of him. "Please don't hurt us."

"You." The pain-filled word made Finn spin around. Berenna stood in the doorway, a woozy looking Brisco behind her. Her voice shook with anger. "You tore my family apart. You took my son from me."

Finn thought about what she didn't say. *Wineon is the one who put her into the position to be used like some disposable toy, over and over again.*

Wineon's eyes went to the slave mark on Berenna's hand. She shook her head, eyes full of fear. "No, no, no. You have it all wrong. I was just doing what Humans First told me to do."

Berenna raised her phaser and fired one shot.

Wineon crumpled to the ground, hand pressed to the wound in her chest. "Help me."

No one moved, and Finn watched the life slowly drain from her eyes. He looked back at Newland and the others. He knew these people were likely just as bad as Wineon had been. He deactivated his visibility and held his phaser up. "You kept Vextonian slaves despite the many warnings Charybdis Station broadcasted across all systems. You will surrender to me now or die."

Newland fell to his knees, arms raised high. "I surrender. Take the Vextonians."

Moyra's form shimmered, then solidified next to him. She held a phaser in each hand. "Slaves and servants to the right of the room. Now!"

By the time the fighting came through the door, Finn had resort members bound and the slaves and servants with the others at the back of the resort.

Crow pushed through the door, eyes scouring the

room until they landed on Finn. "Are you alright?"

Finn smiled widely and kicked Wineon's leg. "Yeah. I am."

———

CROW HELD FINN WRAPPED IN A BLANKET IN HIS ARMS AS they stood at one of the wide windows of the resort. Weber and the other captains had finished securing the resort, and all members were either dead or sitting in cells aboard Charybdis Station ships just like Verulo Malone.

Medics rushed around, tending the wounded. Olivia sat on the ground beside them, wincing as one of the medics bandaged her arm.

"Look." Finn pointed out the window.

Crow looked up and almost swallowed his tongue. A large, fully grown Fire Veil dragon flew over the atmospheric shield. Two smaller dragons flew behind it. Now that the defensive shield was down, the native creatures could move onto the resort grounds. The bright sunshine glinted off the deep red and gold scales of the dragon.

"Isn't it beautiful?" Finn asked, awe in his voice. "One day, Princess Buttercup may be that big."

Olivia groaned. "You mean Princess isn't fully grown yet? General Hackett isn't going to be pleased."

A little boy ran through the room. Marnie chased behind him. "Ezvin, wait. We need to make sure it's safe."

"Mama!"

Berenna pushed away the medic checking her over and fell to her knees. "Ezvin!"

Crow's eyes watered when the boy jumped into his mother's arms and buried his face against her chest crying. "Mama, they said you was dead. They said I had to listen or I'd die too."

Finn pressed his face into Crow's chest. He was shaking, so Crow hugged him tightly. "We found them, Aiden."

"Yeah, we did. You scared ten years off my life though. You were supposed to keep your head down and wait for us."

"I was worried about Brisco." Finn shuddered. "There was some fucked up stuff going on here, Aiden."

"Seriously," Brisco said from his seat nearby. A medic was checking his vitals while they waited for the drug he'd been injected with to wear off. "That woman said she wanted my head for her collection. Who the fuck does shit like that?"

Parker patted his back. "I'm sorry I made you go as a slave instead of a guard."

Crow shook his head. "What's going to happen to this place?"

Finn breathed out slowly. "Now that the galaxy knows about it, we'll do our best to shut it down. All the slaves will be freed and sent to safehouses to recover." Finn looked troubled. "If they can recover."

"What do we do now?" Parker asked, eyes on Berenna and Ezvin.

Crow met Finn's gaze. "We bring the Vextonians home."

20

SILVERLIGHT SYSTEM, PLANET VEXTONAR

row watched all the ships gathered at Vextonar through the viewport of the Blue Albatross. Most were from Charybdis Station's yellow fleet, but other planets and individuals had offered to bring the Vextonians home, and their ships intermeshed with General Shepard's.

Now, they were all gathered outside the atmosphere of the planet. Waiting.

"I don't understand what's happening." Crow turned to Finn. His mate had gotten some much needed rest on the short journey from Fire Veil. He looked like a Charybdis Station lieutenant again, but Crow had to admit he missed the lingerie. *Who am I kidding? I'll get to see it tonight.*

Finn bit his lip and watched as a fleet of Crellic ships approached the planet. "Earth agreed to *remake* Vextonar. I have no idea what that means, but Audre says it's what the planet needs. It can't sustain itself as it is, and there's no economy left to speak of."

Crow made a face. "Remake Vextonar?"

Finn shrugged. "All I know is that Ival and his two Crellic babies are on one of those ships."

Berenna and Ezvin were asleep, curled up together in the captain's chair. Weber didn't seem to mind one bit.

"They're just one family that is about to be reunited." Weber grinned. "Damn, this feels good. Better than any mission I did when we were mercs, that's for sure."

Crow ran a hand over his growing baby bump. It had gotten a little bigger since leaving Rueal, but not by much. Already, he couldn't imagine being separated from Finn and their child. *Even if the tiny jerk inside me keeps making me vomit.*

"One of the Crellic ships is sending a shuttle over," Ignali said, looking up from the communications board. "Should I allow it access?"

"Yes." Weber nodded, looking excited. "I'll go escort a certain human to the bridge."

Crow grinned at Finn. "Should we wake Berenna and Ezvin?"

Finn shook his head. "Where's the fun in that?"

Crow propped his chin on Finn's head. "Roxy keeps hiding my socks."

"She just wants to play with you."

"I think she's building a nest."

Finn gave him an amused look. "She's not going to lay an egg."

Crow made a face. "She'll probably try to hatch more hiss beasts."

His mate pinched his side. "Stop calling her a hiss beast."

They cuddled and teased one another until Weber came back to the bridge. He had a young human with him. Ival pushed a double hover stroller with two big Crellic babies in it.

The man froze when he saw Berenna and Ezvin. A sob tore from his mouth, and he stood there, crying as he watched them sleep.

Finn moved to the stroller. "Go say hello, Ival. I got your two little bits here."

Ival gave him a grateful look then ran to his wife and son. "Berenna, Ezvin."

Berenna's eyes popped open. "Ival? Am I dreaming?"

He fell to his knees next to the chair and hugged her. "Oh gods, Renna."

"Daddy?"

Ival sobbed harder and pulled Ezvin into his arms. "Ez, my boy. I missed you so much."

Crow wiped his eyes and turned away, giving the family some privacy. He looked down at the Crells in the stroller. Finn was already tickling the blue baby's feet.

"This is Yavo," Finn said, laughing with the giggling baby, before tickling the green baby. "And this is Zelea. Aren't they perfect, Aiden? We'll have one of our own soon."

Crow smiled and crouched in front of the stroller.

Zelea grinned at him, her little tusks making her smile even more adorable.

"Yeah, they're perfect."

———

By the next day, the ships outside of Vextonar's atmosphere had tripled. Audre and the others had done what they could to make sure everyone was off planet. Even from space, Vextonar looked empty. It was a city planet whose people had been torn away from it.

"Earth will be the only one on the planet," Finn whispered. "Well, we hope. He said he would try to keep some of the buildings standing but that the planet wanted to be healed."

"What does that mean?" Crow asked.

Finn gave him a flat look. "Again, I don't know what the hell he's talking about."

"He's going to make Vextonar green again," Ival said from behind him. Zelea was perched on his hip, and Ezvin played with Yavo on the floor beside them. Berenna curled into Ival's side.

"Huh?" Crow asked, hating not understanding what was going on.

"Genarg was a barren rock without even an atmosphere." Ival nodded toward the viewport. "Earth brought it back to life. It's a livable planet now. He said Vextonar is calling out to him to heal. It wants to have life again."

"That's not possible," Berenna said, shaking her head.

"You'll see." Ival kissed her head. "It may not be our

home anymore, but I hope Vextonar takes this second chance seriously."

The door to the bridge opened, and General Audre Shepard of the yellow fleet came in. With her were two Vextonians. Crow recognized Abe and Lacey, Dottie's kids.

Abe nodded at him. "I hear you're mated, Crow."

Finn grinned. "He's a lucky man. So, I hear you and Lacey are going to lead Vextonar now."

Abe winced. "Yeah. Unfortunately, we were voted in. Mom was a popular woman, and people trust us because of her."

Crow felt a bit of sympathy for the human. He knew what it was like to live in the shadow of a parent. "You'll do good, Abe. You and Lacey both."

"If we even have a planet to lead," Lacey said. She looked out the window, brow furrowed. "I've heard all the stories and seen the media vids about Earth and the other Crellic Elements, but it's hard to believe he could bring life back to Vextonar. We've had to use atmospheric filters for the past fifty years."

"You'll see." Ival sounded confident. "Give Earth time, and he'll give Vextonar a second chance at life. I never noticed how lacking Vextonar was until I was on Genarg. You're getting a gift, and I hope you are wise enough to take care of it."

"Earth is sending a signal to us and the other ships." Ignali looked over his shoulder, curious. "It's a broadcast."

"Let's see it." Weber nodded and came to stand with Finn and Crow.

The vid-screen flickered and Earth sat before them. The Element was alone in the shuttle. His hair was as tangled as usual and somehow, even after weeks in space, he had soil on his face.

"Hello, Vextonians. You know me as Earth, one of the Crellic Queen's Elements." Earth's expression looked too serious on the face of the young Silet woman he inhabited. "My Queen has caused much harm to this galaxy. With Charybdis Station's help, the worlds she and the other Elements harmed, will be restored. However, I want to help too. Your newly elected leaders, Lacey and Abe, have given me permission to give Vextonar the boost it needs to begin healing."

Abe exchanged a look with Lacey. "Here's to hoping we made the right decision," he said.

Earth narrowed his eyes. "This planet is in agony and close to death. I *will* give it the healing it needs, but if you do not care for it this time, I will come back and take it from you. This is your home and you are responsible for it. Cherish the gifts it gives you. Give me one day."

The screen went blank.

"That was short and ominous." Lacey shivered.

Abe nodded. "He's right, though. Vextonians ruined the planet. If he can do anything for it, then we should honor that by taking better care this time around."

"Can he truly restore the planet though?" Lacey looked doubtful.

"He will." Ival gave them a hard look. "He also meant his threat so don't dismiss him."

They all watched the planet from the viewport for over an hour before people started to wander away, bored and distracted.

"What's Genarg like?" Finn asked Ival.

Ival smiled happily. "The town we've built is in a jungle. The planet itself is about the size of Union Station. It runs on the hot and humid side with plenty of oceans. The wildlife is just now coming back. Earth and the shamans have stayed busy." He looked at his children. "Of course so have the rest of us. There are so many Crellic children and the planet is birthing even more."

"Are there enough people to take care of all the children?" Weber asked, brows raised. "I'm not even going to ask how the planet is birthing babies."

Ival snorted. "I couldn't explain how the birthing works even if you did ask. As for the children, we need more people. Haroon and Xav finally talked Earth into sending announcements to the other planets offering a new start on Genarg to anyone who will help with the children. Haroon told me that they've received plenty of applications and are sorting them now."

Finn smirked. "How is Xav handling being elected governor of Dragon's Hollow?"

Ival laughed. "About as well as you would expect. We can't wait to see what happens when more towns are established and he's promoted to a higher position."

Crow smiled at Finn's laughs. His mate liked to laugh. Something caught his eye and he frowned as he looked out the viewport. "Is that green? There at the center of the planet?"

Quickly, everyone on the bridge gathered back at the viewport.

"That is green," Lacey said, voice full of awe. "There hasn't been that much growth on the planet in generations."

They watched as the green spread, slowly but surely. After another hour the atmosphere of the planet clouded over.

"Clouds? It doesn't rain on Vextonar anymore." Abe's eyes widened. "Gods, what is happening?"

"Maybe it's like terraforming at an accelerated speed," Weber said, amazed.

They watched for hours, but the cloud and gas coverage blocked everything from view. Finn yawned. "I want to see what's happening, but I'm too sleepy."

Lacey struggled to keep her eyes open. "Media is recording it."

"Get some sleep." Finn looked around the bridge. "This won't be a quick process. Rest while you can."

Lacey, Abe, and many of the others left the bridge after a few moments, but Crow was reluctant to leave the viewport.

Finn sighed and tugged him to the captain's chair. "Sit down. We can see perfectly fine from here."

They cuddled together in the chair and Crow's eyes stayed on the clouds swirling around the planet. At some point, Weber brought them blankets and a pillow and Finn fell asleep in Crow's lap, hand resting gently on Crow's abdomen.

The next morning, the sight was the same.

"Earth said one day, right?" Abe asked.

Ival shrugged. "You'll know when he's done."

Two standard days from when Earth arrived, the cloud coverage on Vextonar started to thin out. Crow and Finn were the only ones on the bridge at the time.

"Finn, is that an ocean?" Crow asked.

Finn's mouth dropped open. "That's not one ocean, Aiden. That's two."

"There's so much green." Crow shook his head. "How is this even possible? It takes years to terraform a planet."

They watched as a small shuttle entered the planet's new atmosphere. About an hour later, the shuttle returned to its ship. *Earth finished the job.*

Crow stared at the small, revived planet. "This is a strange galaxy we live in."

Finn gave him an amazed look. "It really is."

A short time later, Crow held Finn's hand and Roxy's leash as they walked off the shuttle. The largest spaceport on Vextonar was still standing, but there was nothing powering it anymore. They had tagged along with the engineers sent to get it up and working again.

Towering trees with indigo bark and deep green leaves towered around the spaceport. Thick, unknown foliage made walking into the forest challenging. The soil was damp and rich, feeding the new plant life all the minerals it needed. A steady rain fell, soaking everything around them.

"Look at this place." Finn looked around in wonder. "All this green. This is what Vextonar was supposed to look like."

"I don't hear birds or insects." Crow frowned. Being

on the ship so long had made him realize how much he took the ambient noise of a planet for granted.

"Vextonar's native species went extinct a long time ago," Ival said. Berenna and he followed behind Crow and Finn.

Roxy stopped to sniff a bush. Her tail swayed back and forth, and her wings fluttered.

"It's going to take work to get the spaceport up and going again," one of the engineers said, shaking his head. "Damn, this is amazing."

Roxy flew up as far as her leash would let her go and sniffed at a lower branch of the nearest tree.

Finn leaned into him. "I'm glad we were here to see this. Parker and Brisco are going to be pissed they stayed behind to finish clearing out the resort on Fire Veil."

"They'll live." Crow watched Finn's ear twitch as the cool breeze tickled it. "The Vextonians have a home to come back to. Where do we go from here, Finn?"

Finn looked up and grinned. "We go to our own home, big guy. We need to transport our Vextonians home, then say goodbye to Dermot and Diana. After that, it's time to go home."

"Home," Crow said, a sense of longing filling him. He was ready to make a home with Finn.

21

ANCHOR'S REST SYSTEM, CHARYBDIS
STATION - FIVE MONTHS LATER

*F*inn hovered around his mate as they walked down the ramp of the Blue Albatross. They had docked at Charybdis Station twenty minutes ago, but Finn hadn't wanted Crow to walk too fast.

"Damn it, Finn, I can walk just fine. I'm pregnant, not dying." Crow glared at him, but Finn kept his eyes on his mate's large baby bump. "You can go ahead. Your friends will all be there. I'll give you all some time."

"They're your friends too." Finn bit his lip. "You just don't know it yet." He wished Brisco and Parker weren't dealing with their belongings. He didn't want Crow to feel left out.

Roxy flew above them, eager to explore Charybdis Station. Finn's darling girl wasn't a baby glimmer anymore. She was over two feet tall and three feet long now. *She still thinks she's a lap cat though.*

"Finn!" Dannol bounced up the ramp, and Finn temporarily forgot his mate.

He hugged Dannol tightly, lifting the slightly smaller man off his feet and spinning him around. "I missed you so much." He didn't want to let go of his friend and buried his face against Dannol's neck, breathing in his familiar scent.

"Missed you too, fuzz butt."

Meggie's voice came from behind them. "Should we be jealous or charmed, Crow?"

"Charmed, I guess. It wouldn't do us any good to be jealous of these two. There's no parting them now." Crow sounded amused.

"Finn!" Hack's voice made Finn look up. His friends and their families all gathered at the bottom of the ramp.

"Did you and Leti adopt more kids?" Finn asked, counting the little ones gathered around Leti and Hack.

Leti rolled his eyes. "No, you just forgot how many there where. Come here and hug me."

Finn pulled Dannol with him, and they both hugged Leti. "I love Leti hugs."

"They're the best," Dannol agreed.

Finn looked over his shoulder. Fasi, Sandve, Amelia, and Draif were surrounding Crow. *Looks like my mate has friends of his own, and he didn't even realize it.*

Morgan and Wyatt got their hugs in next. "It's good to see you back home," Morgan said. "We were worried you would choose Rueal instead."

Finn shook his head. "Charybdis Station will always be home."

"Good." Hack patted his back. "It's been hell staying organized without you. I'm afraid I've made a mess of the training schedules, and I keep forgetting to order plasma grenades."

Finn snickered. "You're hopeless. It's a good thing you're good at leading people and strategy. Otherwise, you'd be a horrible general." Finn tugged on Wyatt's sleeve. "Was Dramacus horrible? All of the Vextonians that were there are back home now."

Wyatt sighed. "It wasn't horrible, but King Xaran is. He's a selfish, narcissistic bastard, though thanks to Dad and I, he's still living."

"Thank you for helping. I know it wasn't easy leaving Estella and the twins." Finn couldn't imagine being apart from his family as long as Wyatt and Morgan had been. The two sacrificed a lot to help others.

Wyatt made a face. "It stinks, and we'll be staying home for a while. It was worth it though."

Finn held a hand over Wyatt's large, pregnant belly and wiggled his brows. Wyatt laughed and nodded permission, so Finn rubbed his hands over Wyatt's baby bump. "I can't wait for my little Hazel to be born."

Morgan wrapped an arm around his shoulder. "Me either. Our son has yet to be named because we can't find the perfect match."

Leti snorted. "You mean you won't compromise, and Wyatt doesn't want to name him Junior."

Finn rolled his eyes and left them bickering. Selene waited for him with her son Xu and her brother Shae. Her face was as emotionless as her voice, but she held her arms out. "Welcome home. I bought you underwear. It's not at all serviceable, but you enjoy fighting in it, so I'm trying to be supportive."

Finn laughed and hugged her. "Gee, thanks. I missed you, Selene. Hey, Xu."

"Hey," Xu said, grinning. His eyes widened. "Mom, why are your horns wiggling?"

Selene stood frozen in place, eyes slightly widened. "My horns are vibrating."

Shae's eyes widened, and he started grinning. "Sweet gods, is this really happening?"

"Okay?" Finn exchanged a look with Xu. "What's going on?"

Selene tilted her head and looked around the dock. She almost seemed to be following her vibrating horns as she moved around boxes and dodged people.

Finn and Xu followed behind her, curious about what was happening. Shae practically cackled as he ran after them.

Selene stopped when Parker started down the ramp of the ship, hands full of bags. "Who is that man?"

"His name is Parker." Finn started to grin. "Shae, how do Sirens find their mates?"

"One of two ways." Shae looked smug. "Either we sing our mates to us, or our horns lead us to them."

"He's a Dedril like me," Xu said quietly, eyes full of hope. "Is he Mom's mate? Will he like me?"

Shae hugged his nephew. "If he's worth anything, he will."

Finn waved Beck over. The large Grell picked him up in a hug. "We missed you, Finn. Do you want to see my babies?"

Finn laughed. "Of course I do, but first, look at Selene. I think Aiden's friend Parker is her mate."

Beck dropped him to his feet and spun around. "Say what? Who is this Parker guy? What makes him think he's good enough for Selene? Hack! Selene's mate is a stranger." He charged toward Hack, face thunderous.

Xu giggled. "Oh, no."

Finn rolled his eyes. "Hey, Beol."

Beck's mate nodded. "Hello."

"Still stiff and unfriendly, I see." Finn hid his smile.

"Still fluffy tailed and annoying, I see." Beol didn't bother to try and hide his grin. "Hack really does need you home. I've had to listen to him whine at every budget meeting because he keeps overspending."

Alois picked him up in a hug before Finn could reply. "Finn boy, you're finally home. Juniper, Icarus, and Ma are cooking up a welcome home meal at Leti's house. I'm hungry."

Finn rolled his eyes. "Is that your way of saying we need to move this to Leti's?"

"Yes. My mate is back home with most of the babies too, and I miss them." Alois grinned, then tilted his head. "Why is Selene staring at that guy like that?"

"I think it's her way of trying to seduce him." Shae rubbed his chin. "I'm not sure, but he looks a little scared."

"Parker really is a good guy," Finn said. "Brisco, there, I don't know about, but Parker is good."

Brisco made a rude gesture as he walked past. "I heard that, Finny. Where's Death? I need him to check out my soul."

Beol blinked as he watched Brisco. "Now I realize why Death decided to stay home today."

Finn finished hugging his friends, then pulled Crow onto the shuttle tram. "What do you think of Charybdis Station?"

Crow shook his head as he stared out the tram window. "Amazing."

Finn turned around, curious what had caught Crow's eye. Princess Buttercup flew high above the tram. A much smaller Fire Veil dragon flew beside him. *That must be Pepper's dragon Aagy.* Finn could barely see the shapes of Honey and Stardust, the baby dragons riding on Princess's head.

A flutter of movement closer to the tram caught his attention. "Roxy?" Finn asked, then laughed. His glimmer flew alongside Sebastian's bird, Mustachio. They almost looked like they were racing.

As the tram slowed at their stop, a few fairy-like Charybdis Fyrelings flew past the window, pausing to wave hello, before moving on. "I heard about those, but damn." Crow shook his head.

When the tram stopped and they all unloaded, Gravy, Biscuit, and Peri barked and ran up to meet them.

Finn knelt to pet each of the dogs and was instantly buried in wet, slobbery kisses.

Dr. Bloop stopped by for a quick lick to Finn's face and woofed hello before moving to Beck's side. Gravy and Peri's puppy wore his usual Blue Solace vest and had his work goggles perched on his head.

Luna, Sebastian and Alois's dog, ran past them

followed by a pack of unfamiliar puppies that looked a lot like Gravy and Peri. *Hack's newest batch of grandpuppies.*

"Was that a pig?" Crow's head turned to watch Porkchop running from Fluffle, Selene's cat.

"Yep. There's Dannol's rooster, Hector. The hen next to him is Miss Speckles. She belongs to Juniper."

Crow shook his head. "Welcome home, right?"

"There are a lot of pets in the neighborhood." Finn hugged his mate. "Pets and kids."

Sami and his friend Almond ran past them. Pax, Sami's Betonize hunting cat, followed behind them, eyes looking for trouble.

Crow gave Finn a slow smile. "A whole lot of pets and kids."

An hour later, Crow was settled in a chair in Leti's backyard with his feet propped up and a plate of food resting on his stomach. Finn brought him another drink and took a moment to admire his mate. *I'm a lucky man.*

"I can't believe they have a llama and two goats living in their backyard." Crow shook his head and glared at Trixie. "You can't have my food, Trixie. Go chew on the table again."

Trixie gave him a pitiful look and Crow sighed before handing the goat a bit of celery.

Finn hummed happily. Dannol was sitting next to him with Meggie while Nessa ran around with the other children. His mate was happy and well fed on his other side, and all his friends were home and healthy. *Life is good.*

"Juniper and Tempest are going to have a wedding in a few months. Ma and Sybil are at war over the color scheme." Dannol giggled. Finn's friend loved gossip. "Juniper and Tempest don't care and I think they took a bet to see which mother will win."

"They all get along at the diner, right?" Finn asked, feeling a bit of panic at the idea of not getting to eat at Juniper's because someone burned it down in a fit of rage.

"Oh yeah." Dannol nodded, grinning. "Gloria works there and she keeps everything under control. She used to live on Vextonar but wanted to come here. Icarus was thinking about working with Juniper too, but Juny said he ought to open his own diner in Full Moon's territory. He even said he'd help him set it up."

"That's great." Finn slid a few pieces of his chicken onto Crow's plate. "What about the daycare?"

"Shae's place is doing well." Dannol snorted. "I told him he has serious job security in this neighborhood."

"For real," Finn said, snickering.

Crow smacked his arm. "No laughing since baby Hazel here is part of that job security."

Finn snuggled into his side. "Good point. What other gossip do you have?"

"Leti is working on establishing a university here on the station" Dannol tapped his chin. "We have a lot of medical research internships, but the Lord Admiral never considered a university before."

"Mom and Councilman Delino are living together now too." Meggie gave them a sly look. Meggie hugged Dannol. The Bracken looked as stylish as ever in her dark blue pantsuit. Beck and the others had fully restored her features to their original appearance, but Finn knew that wasn't where her beauty came from. *I'm glad Dannol found her.* "I gave her some panties like Finn's and she about died of embarrassment."

Finn couldn't be upset about that. *Everyone needs pretty things.*

"Sebastian's new apprentice is improving. Leti keeps trying to talk Sebastian into training shamans at the university when it's up and going." Dannol yawned. "Oh, and Quinn and Cordelia are getting married."

"What? Seriously?" Finn looked across the yard and smiled when he saw Cordelia and Quinn playing cards with Brisco. "That's great."

"Do Sirens have a courting ritual or something?" Crow arched a brow. "If not, I think someone needs to explain that weapons aren't romantic."

Selene was showing Parker her favorite vibroblade, and to be fair, Parker *did* look interested. "Let her do things her way," Finn said, propping his chin on his fist. "They'll figure it out."

Fire ran over to him. The Element had Jellybean on his shoulder as usual. "I didn't get to hug you!"

"I know. We've been here hours." Finn had begun to wonder if Fire was going to be able to pull himself away from the food table.

Fire sat on Crow's other side and joined in their snuggling. "Hi, Crow. It's nice to meet you in person. Roxy likes you, so I'm sure I will too." Fire turned his gaze on Finn. "I'm glad you're home. I need to talk to you about your underwear. I have questions."

Fasi stood up near the back door of Leti and Hack's home. "Can I have everyone's attention?"

Thank you, catnip gods. Finn ignored Fire's annoyed look and focused on the Lord Admiral.

Fasi looked around the yard with a fond look. "There are a few things I want to say and now is as good a time as any. The events of the last few years have been equal parts horrific and wonderous. A few years ago, my son found his mate. While I was beyond happy for him, I never realized what incredible pride I would feel for them both for their character and actions. They have led us in victory against Humans First and the Crellic Queen in their own unique way." He smiled as he watched his grandchildren playing with the pets in the yard. "They have a wildly beautiful family that brings me such joy, and Leti's capacity to love has brought my station so many remarkable new citizens. Thank you, sons."

Leti wiped his eyes and smiled wide. He leaned against Hack. The two men shared a happy look with the Lord Admiral.

Fasi nodded at Morgan and Wyatt. "As happy as I am about Leti coming into our lives, I'm also happy for the other mates that have joined the Blue Solace family. Wyatt, you make our pretty boy Morgan so happy and offer us all your steady, intelligent counsel. Your caring nature and sheer determination to help others is an asset to my station. Thank you for making this your home."

Wyatt looked shocked. He looked at their twins, Kiki and Pela. The girls were playing in the sandbox with Pepper and Aagy. "This is our home. I can't imagine living anywhere else now."

Morgan took his hand and kissed it. "That's the truth."

Fasi smiled fondly at them, then turned to Sebastian and Alois. "My dearest Sebastian, your bravery is a shining light to all of us. Your personal strength and intelligence are extraordinary. In addition to that, you make our Alois a wonderful mate and I love how you truly appreciate him. You both know how lucky you are."

Sebastian sniffed and leaned against Alois. He held their youngest, Mordy, on his lap. Their eldest, Nina, was currently giggling and chasing Luna with some of the other children.

"Thanks, Lord Admiral," Alois said gruffly. "It took a little time to get here, but we're home now."

Fasi grinned. "That you are." He turned to Beck and Beol. "Home and family have always been important to Charybdis Station. Beck, you and the Brackenstones have been the heart of this station for a long time. That genius, creative mind of yours has brought us the Bracken and the Charybdis Fyrelings. That's a perfect match for our Full Moon general. Beol, you and your people have saved our asses more than once. We're proud to add your integrity and skill to our station. We're also pretty damn happy that you keep our Beckie Boo smiling."

Beck groaned and buried his face into baby Aketil's hair. The little Crell sat in his lap, happily stuffing food into her mouth. "Don't embarrass us."

Beol held one of the twins in his arms. Nidi looked a lot like Beck with mostly Grell features. Their other son, Bren, was in Ma Brackensone's lap. Bren was the smallest of their children and his face was as grumpy as Beol's.

Fasi laughed and moved his attention to Draif. "Fine. I'll talk about our Draify Loo."

Draif moaned and leaned his head back, staring at the atmospheric shield above them. "Why are people still calling me that?"

"Because we love you," Ma said, smiling wide.

Fasi nodded. "We do love you, Draif. You bring a strong will and determination to this station that truly humbles me. I am honored to work beside you. The fact that you are mated to our Lucas only makes us love you more. You two support each other in a way few couples do."

Lucas wrapped an arm around Draif and nodded. "Thank you, sir."

Fasi turned to look at Finn and Crow. "Now, we have another couple to admire. Finn, I've loved you since the day my son brought you into his crew. I knew you were smart and capable, but until now, I never realized how utterly persistent you are. I am proud of what you and Crow have accomplished over the last year. Thank you both for choosing Charybdis Station."

Finn shared a look with Crow. His mate looked as stunned as he felt. Finn smiled slowly at Fasi. "This is our home. Charybdis Station and what it stands for is worth fighting for."

Fasi grinned. "It really is." He looked back around at

all the people gathered. "Together, we've defeated a coalition bent on subjugating the galaxy and an ancient being determined to sow as much chaos as she could. Rueal and Vextonar are being remade into stronger, more tolerant worlds because of our actions. I am proud of each and every one of you. Without you, the galaxy would be a dark place of pain and suffering. We've helped save whole worlds and reunite families. I can't think of a better accomplishment."

———

A FEW HOURS LATER, FINN AND CROW FINALLY MADE IT home. Finn's small house was now a two-story home with well-tended Rueal sundrop roses lining the front. Finn noticed a Roxy sized hammock and cat perch to the right of the walk.

"This is our home?" Crow asked.

Finn leaned against his mate and stroked across his stomach. "This is our home. Let's go in and see how many druffle we got stuck with."

AUTHOR'S NOTE

The Rebel's Mate is the last book in The Blue Solace series. However, I love this book universe too much to leave it, so there will be three spin-off series. One is called Charybdis Station and will be shorter sci/fi-fantasy romance books focused on couples at Charybdis Station. *Death's Mate, Rune and Silas,* and *Fire's Mate* will be the first three. The second series is called The Green Solace and will follow Cas and his fleet as they help the worlds destroyed by the Queen and her Elements. The last series is called the Crellic Revival. It is a trilogy of novels that will explore what is happening on Genarg. I hope you enjoyed The Blue Solace as much as I did and join me in my new series.

ALSO BY C.W. GRAY

The Blue Solace Series – science fiction/fantasy, mpreg

1. The Mercenary's Mate – https://amzn.to/2MAOFEH
2. The General's Mate – https://amzn.to/2G1abRE
3. The Soldier's Mate – https://amzn.to/2S7R6ng
4. The Lieutenant's Mate – https://amzn.to/2THZ47w
5. The Engineer's Mate – https://amzn.to/2HpI4vH
6. The Captain's Mate – https://amzn.to/2knP03W
7. The Rebel's Mate –

Charybdis Station – science fiction/fantasy, mpreg, spin-off

1. Death's Mate – *Coming Soon*
2. Rune and Silas – *Coming Soon*
3. Fire's Mate – *Coming Soon*

The Hobson Hills Omegas – non-shifter, mpreg, omegaverse

1. Falling for the Omega – https://

amzn.to/2BgWURV
2. Snow Kisses for My Omega – https://amzn.to/2TdDiol
3. Romancing the Omega – https://amzn.to/2UNENKD
4. Healing the Omega – https://amzn.to/2FNcXrY
5. A Pint for my Omega – https://amzn.to/2XItQf7
6. Unraveling the Omega – https://amzn.to/2xRCnRL
7. The Alpha's Christmas Wish – https://amzn.to/2qXkGAl
8. Convincing the Alpha – *Coming Soon*

Hobson Hills Shorts – short stories from the world of Hobson Hills Omegas

1. The Beta's Love Song – https://amzn.to/2UrRPNN
2. Bennett's Dream – https://amzn.to/2GwSpG3
3. Justin's Journey – https://amzn.to/2DhW1t1
4. Grey's Gift – https://amzn.to/2BcjxXf
5. Hobson Hills Shorts: Volume One – https://amzn.to/2M3oGGZ

Holiday Omegas Shorts – holiday short stories from the world of The Silver Isles – paranormal, mpreg

1. Cauldron Cake Pops and a Witch's Kiss –

https://amzn.to/33wMrhc
2. Sugar Cookies and a Witch's Love – https://amzn.to/2NE4CeJ
3. Candy Hearts and a Witch's Ring – *Coming in February, 2020*

The Silver Isles – paranormal, mermen, mpreg

1. The Guppy Prince – https://amzn.to/2q9Q8en
2. The Not so Little Merman – *Coming Soon*
3. The Sea Witch – *Coming Soon*

If you would like to keep up with releases, please like and follow me on Instagram (@c.w._gray) or Facebook (@cwgrayauthor), join C.W. Gray's Reading Nook on Facebook, or visit my website at https://cwgray-author.com.

EXCERPT

Unedited excerpt from *Death's Mate*, a book in the Charybdis Station series.

Death held Kiki in his lap as he sat in the comfortably cushioned chair in his study. His granddaughter leaned back against him trustingly as they read from the children's book on his tablet.

This could have been Wyatt and I. He had dreamed of holding his son in his arms just like this. Of course he had usually been quickly distracted by a new puzzling virus to explore.

"Grandad, do voices." Kiki looked up at him, eyes big and hopeful.

Voices? Panic started to fill him. His youngest grandchildren were only now starting to speak coherently, but they hadn't asked for specific things like a *story* and *voices* before. His eldest grandchild, Estella, was much easier to deal with. She wanted to be a doctor, so her questions made perfect sense.

"Grandad?" Kiki's lip trembled and Death almost whimpered. As Verion Morrick, he was very lacking in the parenting department. As Death, he had zero experience with children. Both halves that formed his whole were completely useless here.

A low laugh drew his attention to the door. Val leaned against it, broad face smiling. The Betonize man's presence had an instant impact on Death's peace of mind.

"Hey, Kiki. Can I do the voices?" Val smiled wide, sharp fangs gleaming. It should have been intimidating, but Kiki knew Val well.

"Val, yes pees." She clapped. "Do moo cow voice."

Val's laughing eyes met his. "Care if I intrude on story time, Very?"

Ha! Death and Verion Morrick were one in all things Val. "You are never an intrusion."

EXCERPT

Excerpt from *Falling for the Omega*– Book One in the Hobson Hills Omegas Series

Carter loaded the last of his tools into his new work van and shut the door. His first day in his new profession was off to a good start. He had three clients to see today and eight spread out during the rest of the week.

Finally getting his plumbing license had been a good idea, even if his perfect, wealthy family hated the idea of him being a plumber.

Hell, they had also hated the idea of him being a soldier and of him moving out of state when he came back injured. They pretty much hated every decision he made.

The crisp fall wind was cold, but the gold, brown, and red leaves on the trees and ground made the cold worth dealing with. Autumn in Maine sure wasn't the same as autumn in Georgia, but so far, he was damn happy with the move. There was a peace here amongst the trees that he hadn't managed to find anywhere else.

"Hi, Mr. Neighbor!"

A child's voice came from behind him, startling Carter. He spun around, stumbling a bit on his prosthesis, and faced the little girl standing a few feet from his van.

She looked about five or six, with two black braids, caramel skin, and a freckled nose. When she smiled brightly, he saw a small gap between her two front teeth.

A black and gray miniature schnauzer sat at her feet, gaze stern and trained on him.

He looked around and didn't see any adults. His little half acre tract was quite a ways back from the road, nestled between a good-sized apple orchard on one side and a thick forest on the other.

Where the hell had this little girl come from?

"My name's Olive, and I brought you a welcome basket. I made it myself, but Daddy made you one too. He's gonna bring it tonight. I wanted you to get mine first, 'cause it's from me and then we'll be best friends." The little girl paused to take a breath. Her wide brown eyes sparkled and met his straight on, innocent and fearless. "We'll be best friends forever."

She didn't even seem to see the scars along the side of his face. The burn marks had already made two kids cry at the grocery store yesterday. Both times, the parents had been too embarrassed to apologize. They just grabbed their kids and ran.

"Uh, where's your daddy, Olive?" His voice was

deep and cracked, broken by the scarring on his neck. Her adoring stare was starting to freak him out a little. He'd never really been around kids.

"He's at home," she answered and handed him the basket. "See what I brought you? Look, look, look."

"Do you know your phone number? Maybe we could give your daddy a call," Carter said, taking the basket from Olive. He pulled the small hand towel from the top and almost dropped the basket. "Is that a hedgehog?"

"Yep! That's Hodges the hedgehog. He wanted to come visit too. Oh and this is Winston," she said and knelt to pet the small dog.

"Okay, your number?" He tried to keep his gruff voice kind. No sense in scaring the kid.

"Olive! Olive Persephone Wilson! Where are you?" A man's voice called from the orchard, full of panic and desperation.

"Uh oh," Olive said. She hurriedly looked around, then darted behind his van, Winston following her. "That's Daddy." She poked her head out and stared hard. "Tell. Him. Nothing."

She quickly hid again when a young omega rushed out of the orchard. He was her father, had to be. He looked just like her.

Carter suddenly couldn't catch his breath. The man in front of him was simply adorable. He was short and well formed, a little chubby. His black hair fell in curls around his face, and his wide hazel eyes contrasted beautifully with his caramel skin. The same freckles that decorated his daughter's nose, fell across his own.

Where it looked cute on the kid, on her father... Bad thoughts, Carter! Bad thoughts!

"Have you seen a little girl? Black hair? Brown eyes? Miniature schnauzer with her? Maybe a hedgehog?"

Carter stared at the handsome man, mouth gaping, for too long.

The man frowned at him, tilting his head. "Are you alright?" His shy smile revealed the small gap between his front teeth.

Oh fuck, he was so damn perfect. He met Carter's eyes too, didn't even glance at the scars.

"Mister?"

Carter shook his head and did his best to pull himself together. He smiled, as best he could with the scar tissue, and nodded toward the van, holding a finger to his lips, encouraging the man to keep quiet.

Olive's father rolled his eyes and stomped around the van. A squealing Olive ran from her hiding spot and hid behind Carter, hugging him around the waist.

"Mr. Neighbor, save me!" Her giggling told him she wasn't too worried about her father catching her.

"Olive, you scared me to death running off like that." Her father really did look worried. "What have I told you about leaving the house without me?"

"But daddy," she whined. "I wanted to meet Mr. Neighbor. We're best friends now, and I gave him a welcome basket. I was being hospital."

Carter frowned. Hospital?

"Hospitable, baby girl, and it doesn't matter. You are too little to be wandering around by yourself and talking to strangers. No television time this week, and you have to clean out Pooka and Banjo's stalls on Saturday."

Olive gave a big sigh and leaned her forehead into Carter's leg. "Okay, Daddy, but it was worth it. I have a new best friend now."

The man met Carter's stare, a question in his eyes. Carter nodded and gave his best half smile.

"Well, maybe our new neighbor would like to come over for dinner one night? So that we can meet him properly," the man said.

"Yay! Mr. Neighbor, can you come tonight? Daddy's gonna make apple dumplins for dessert."

Carter smiled at the little girl and nodded. "Yeah, if it's okay with your dad."

The man smiled and nodded eagerly. "That would be great. I hardly ever get to cook for anyone but Olive." He gave a flustered look and held out his hand. "Oh, I forgot. My name is Elijah Wilson. I live in the farmhouse with the orchard. Of course, you've met Olive."

Carter shook his hand, touch lingering longer than it should. He was reluctant to release him but finally did. "Yeah, I'm Carter Benson. Just moved here from Georgia."

"Wow, so Maine's probably a bit different, huh?"

"Yeah, but all the colors on the trees? And ya'll actually have snow. I've never seen much of it."

"You say that like snow is a good thing." Elijah shuddered. "Well, welcome to Hobson Hill. I see Olive already gave you a welcome basket."

Carter looked back in it. "There's a hedgehog in

there." His coarse voice was getting rougher as he spoke. He wasn't used to talking so much. Doctors said it was good for him to do though.

"I put cider in there for you. It's in my favorite big girl cup, the one with Moana. There's also butter from Pooka and some of Daddy's bread. It's so yummy!"

"Thanks, Olive. I appreciate it," Carter said. The little girl still hung on his leg, smiling up at him. She was a cute one, he acknowledged, even though she was clearly a little crazy. It was a good crazy though.

"Your alpha won't mind me coming," Carter asked Elijah.

The man winced and lowered his eyes. "I don't have an Alpha, so no, that won't be a problem."

Carter was surprised. Happy, but surprised. This adorable man had to be beating them off with a stick. Of course, some folks thought poorly about single omegas, and some alphas refused to even speak to them. Idiots.

"I guess I'll see you tonight. What time?"

"Oh, is six okay?" Elijah's confidence seemed to bounce back at Carter's question.

"That's fine. I better get to work."

"Yes, of course," Elijah said and pulled Olive off Carter's leg. "Come on, Olive. We better get back to the house. We need to get you to school."

"Okay. Bye, Carter, love you!" The little girl and her dog ran off through the orchard.

"I swear it's exhausting keeping up with her," Elijah sighed. Carter smiled and held the hedgehog out to him. "Thanks," he said, taking Hodges and smiling shyly. "See you tonight. Have a good day at work."

Carter stood frozen as he watched Elijah walk away. He was in trouble. Big, wonderful trouble.

Buy Here: My Book

EXCERPT

Excerpt from *The Guppy Prince*, book one in The Silver Isles.

Dover Rees floated in the deepest part of his creek, enjoying the rushing sound of the waterfall to his right. Sunlight filtered through the water, glinting off the deep blue of his guppy tail. His thin and delicate caudal fin spread out like an elegant fan, dancing through the warm water as he swayed.

His favorite smooth and colorful pebbles were strewn around below him, and he admired the shells he had collected and placed beside them. Dover breathed deeply and enjoyed the peace and quiet. No one mocked him or bossed him around. No one watched him with cold eyes and hidden smirks. *I wish I could stay here forever.*

Sudden movement beside him jarred him from his thoughts and he laughed when Chubber grabbed a bright pink stone in his small brown paws and swam away. Dover's otter friend liked to steal Dover's shinies then share them with him again later.

A brook trout swam past him and Dover debated grabbing it for an early lunch, but he wasn't too hungry yet. Lately, he'd been eating less and less, and he couldn't make himself care.

The quiet water around him hummed as Nami quickly swam to him. His best friend's guppy tail was a lovely pink pattern with black dots, and her short black hair floated around her head. The cat with a mermaid tail on her black tankini top made him smile. He loved her purr-maid shirts.

"Have you eaten today, Your Highness?" she asked.

Dover scowled. "Don't call me that."

"When you're acting like a pouting asswipe, that's what you get called." Nami wrapped her arms around him and settled her head on his shoulder. "What's wrong with you, Dover?"

Dover had no answer for her. All he knew was he felt empty inside and it was harder and harder to get up in the morning. "I think I ate some bad clams."

"Every day for the past two months?" Nami leaned back and glared at him, her dark eyes seeing right through him.

Chubber came to his rescue, swimming in between them and wrapping his lean body across Dover's shoulders. "Chubber wants to get a snack."

Nami sighed, bubbles filling the water around her. "Mom is in your cottage making lunch. You're worrying us, bluetail."

Dover stroked a hand through her hair, then shoved

her down and pushed up, swimming toward the surface.

"Damn it!" Nami swam after him.

He laughed, heart warming. *Someone cares about me.* It wasn't his family, but Nami and her mom were closer to him than his parents or any of his twelve siblings.

Chubber clung to his back and nibbled on his ear until he mentally apologized. Chubber cared about him the most.

His creek was deep, but it didn't take him long to reach the surface. Shauna waited for them on the shore, hands on her hips. Chubber's mother, Shell, stood on her hind legs beside the mermaid, chirping loudly. Uh oh. He really was in trouble.

"You didn't eat breakfast, did you?" The wind blew strands of Shauna's pink hair across her face, ruining her glare.

"Sorry, Shauna."

She sighed. "I made your favorite."

"Grilled shrimp salad?" Dover's stomach rumbled.

"With avocado, papaya, mango, and pineapple. All your favorites." Shauna gave him a soft look. "Come eat, bluetail."

Dover summoned his human legs and a few seconds later, walked out of the creek, naked, with Chubber clinging to his shoulder. Shauna handed him a deep teal sarong, and he tied it about his waist.

Shell crawled up his leg and into his arms, then rubbed her slick furry face against his. She was a bit heavier than Chubber, but he was still a baby.

"Why does he get all the loving?" Nami asked, grumbling as she tied a sarong around her own waist.

Dover chuckled when Shauna arched an eyebrow at her daughter. "Did you say something, sweetness?"

"No, ma'am," Nami said, wincing.

"You two come eat lunch." Shauna turned around and walked toward Dover's large cottage.

Dover closed his eyes for a moment and savored the feel of the moss-covered rocks under his feet, and the comfortable breeze quickly drying his curly blue hair. He loved his home so much. It was his sanctuary.

Buy Here: https://amzn.to/2q9Q8en